West Side Stories

ALSO FROM CITY STOOP PRESS

New Chicago Stories
edited by Fred L. Gardaphè

South Side Stories
(forthcoming)
edited by Steve Bosak

West Side Stories

edited by
George Bailey

City Stoop Press

Chicago

1992

Grateful acknowlegment is made to the following:

Tony Ardizonne, "Nonna": copyright 1986 by Tony Ardizonne. Reprinted from *The Evening News*, published by University of Georgia Press.

Rochelle Distelheim, "Home Movies": copyright 1977 by Rochelle Distelheim. Reprinted by permission of *McCalls*.

Aaron Freeman, "Acoustic Catholicism": copyright 1990 by Aaron Freeman. Reprinted by permission of *The Chicago Tribune*.

James McManus, "Making It Talk": copyright 1990 by James McManus. Appeared originally in *Formations*, Vol. 5, No. 3.

Cover photograph © 1992 by Stephen Marc. Photo location: Garfield Park Field House, 100 North Central Park, Chicago, Illinois

Cover design by Midge Stocker and Loraine Edwalds
Interior design by Midge Stocker
Typeset by MS Editorial Service, Chicago, Illinois
     text in Sabon 11.5/13.5

City Stoop Press
4317 N. Wolcott
Chicago, Illinois 60613

LC 91-077074

ISBN 0-9627425-1-1

Contents

Acknowledgments

This book was partially funded through a Faculty Development Grant from Columbia College, Chicago. I would like to thank the Chicago Park District for permitting the use of a photograph of the Garfield Park Field House, 100 N. Central Park Avenue, Chicago, IL 60624, for the cover design. I am indebted to the staff of Special Collections at the Harold Washington Library for providing background information about the West Side.

Thanks to Fred Gardaphé, K.J. Zarker, Linda Bailey and Mark Boone for reading and commenting on various manuscripts. A warm and special thanks to Karen Lee Osborne who saw the need for this book and whose inspiration helped to make it a reality.

Introduction

The West Side of Chicago is a geographical location and a state of mind. In 1970, a few months after Fred Hampton and Mark Clark were killed at 2337 Monroe, my parents bought a building in "K-Town," in West Garfield Park.

During the mid-1950s, my parents, like thousands of displaced black sharecroppers fleeing the south, saw Chicago as a city which offered a better life, and a better education for their children. After living on the Near North Side for several years, without any real connection to the community in which they lived, my parents moved to West Garfield Park. After all, their church was there on Grenshaw Street, and many of the people with whom they shared a common background lived in these communities. In retrospect, these events take on new and powerful significance for me. I see that, unlike the myth of the missing African-American family man, my father and thousands of others like him *chose* to set down their roots in this tumultuous yet enduring place.

The nine communities making up the West Side are: Humboldt Park, West Town, the Near West Side, East Garfield Park, West Garfield Park, Austin, North Lawndale, South Lawndale, and the Lower West Side. These communities are bounded on the north by the C.M. & ST. P. & P. Railroad, Kinzie Street, and the Chicago and Northwestern Railroad, on the south by the Chicago Sanitary and Ship Canal, the Chicago River, and the Adlai E. Stevenson Expressway, on the immediate west by Oak Park and Cicero, and on the east by the Chicago River.

The development of Chicago as a city of national prominence and importance owes much to the contributions of the people who have lived and currently live in West Side communities. American industries grew out of these communities.

The McCormick Reaper Company moved to the Lower West Side in 1873 and built a plant at 27th Street and Western, which set the stage for economic growth on the West Side for the coming century. During the first two decades of the twentieth century, the West Side of Chicago, especially the Lower West Side (Pilsen) and South Lawndale, enjoyed a robust industrial base.

The Irish, German, Italian, Polish, Scandinavian, Jewish, Czechoslovakian, Lithuanian and Ukrainian immigrants who lived and worked in West Side communities have all repeated a pattern of moving in, acquiring wealth and moving on to better prospects. West Side neighborhoods and communities continue to reverberate with impressions and flavors left by European ethnic groups.

The latest arrivals to West Side communities, African-Americans and Latinos, are currently faced with the tasks of resuscitating and reinvigorating the commercial and cultural facets of these neighborhoods and communities.

Whenever I travel through some West Side neighborhoods, I feel as though I'm on an anthropological/archeological expedition through disquieting strata of urban America. During these journeys I excavate collective impressions of past and present-day life on these streets. Each new level reveals stories—artifacts etched on the faces of people and the facades of buildings—terrible and beautiful, rich and dense.

Traveling east from the Garfield Park Field House, on Central Park Avenue, along Warren Boulevard, partially obscured by smog, one sees the glass and steel edifices of downtown Chicago tower over abandoned and deteriorating buildings, neat, compact bungalows and empty lots sprinkled with broken glass. Along Division, Chicago, Lake, Washington, Madison, Jackson, Roosevelt and Cermak, stories from the past and present speaks from stoops, backyards and barstools. Move south toward the Lower West Side and South Lawndale, along Halsted, Ashland, Western, California, Kedzie, Pulaski, Kostner and Cicero, and see the factories, once productive, now silent repositories of debris.

I have walked down main arteries and neighborhood streets where an inordinate number of people, especially black and Latino men, sit the days away, eyes averted, waiting for something to happen. They appear on stoops and on street corners, and in warmer weather, under trees, sitting on cast-off furniture. They are men, women and children still waiting to stand in the promise and bounty of "trickle down" and "a thousand points of light." They constitute the faceless, rapidly spreading urban underclass, left behind, without work, caught up in a system which has rendered them null and void.

During the months that I have spent assembling this anthology, I have had the privilege of meeting and listening to many West Siders. As I sat in Mexican and Soul Food restaurants in South Lawndale and in West Garfield Park, I listened to laborers, students, business people and gangbangers, people who are long-time and short-time West Side residents. I have heard the bittersweet stories of "the old neighborhood" from Jewish-Americans who once lived in North Lawndale. I've chatted with people gardening, repairing their homes, people who see beyond the blight affecting West Side neighborhoods. I come away from this experience immeasurably enriched and strengthened by people who have been willing to share with me their past, their hopes for the future, their dreams and their realities.

One need only glance at some of the neighborhoods making up the West Side of Chicago to know that they are among the poorest urban areas in America. Many residents of these communities feel that they have been abandoned by all forms of government. From neighborhood to neighborhood and street to street, the proof of the dearth of care is evident.

Some West Side neighborhoods are alive with the mandate to, as a woman on the Cicero bus said, "make it better." Despite the behavior of fearful motorists, who drive quickly through West Side neighborhoods with locked doors and rolled up windows, the woman on the Cicero bus wants these people to know that people on the West Side are not all "dope fiends." She wants to tell people who do not know the West Side that strong families with values and goals are at work building neighborhoods.

I have come to understand that although several West Side neighborhoods are indeed economically and culturally isolated, citizens of these neighborhoods do not see themselves as losers, written off in real or make-believe genocidal plots.

Rather, many see themselves as key players in long-term, grass-roots movements which sputter and falter, yet continue to forge ahead with small, often intangible victories.

For example, a vacant lot, now the venue of dope dealers, is all that remains of the building where in 1966 Martin Luther King, Jr., lived when he headed the Union to End Slums Movement. The building he repaired is gone, but adjacent to the lot is a youth center, at 1530 S. Hamlin, where dedicated community workers and volunteers offer tutoring programs, parenting classes and support services.

Bethel New Life and other Community Development Corporations (CDCs) have made a powerful commitment to helping neighborhoods solve problems. In *Rebuilding the Walls: A Nuts and Bolts Guide to the Community Development Methods of Bethel New Life, Inc. in Chicago*, a book put out by Bethel New Life, this Lutheran Church organization sets forth a framework for helping people living in West Garfield improve the quality of life in their neighborhoods. The Bethel approach stresses three fundamental concepts: "Self-help," "Partnerships" and "Wholistic Development." Helping people to realize the reaffirming power of their cultural history is a critical component in Bethel's mission.

Another positive force for change is Por Un Barrio Mejor (For a Better Neighborhood), 2406 S. Mallard in South Lawndale. This organization concentrates on drop-out prevention, parenting training and advocacy for school reform in Chicago Public Schools.

Dr. Pedro Albizu Campos Puerto Rican High School, 1671 N. Claremont, in the West Town

community, is known by two other names: Centro
Latino, and The Puerto Rican Cultural Center. It
grew out of the determination of the community to
address the needs of Puerto Rican students who
suffer crunching self-esteem problems in Chicago
public schools. The school's mission is to raise whole
and productive people who must negotiate, even
when difficult, the gifts and the inequalities of a
complex America.

Those who have despaired in the belief that
grass-roots movements are a thing of the past need
only visit the West Side and attend a block club
meeting, a black businessmen's association meeting
in Austin, or listen to the talk of people having
breakfast at Betty's Fine Foods at 4422 W. Madison.
A grouping of tables near the door is always taken
up with a contingent of religious leaders from the
neighborhood. The morning discussions always
include ideas about how to improve the area.

The West Side of Chicago is emerging as a political
crucible for forging positive gains in wards and
districts where political intelligence is confounded by
the magnitude and complexity of existing problems;
we have problems for which we have no models for
solving.

I harbor disturbing notions that certain West Side
neighborhoods have been blacked out; that the full
spectrum of the world does not enter into these
places; that people living in these neighborhoods
have difficulty accessing, interpreting and applying
the bounty of useful information the world has to
offer to better their lives—leaving them farther and
farther behind. My ability to drive away from the
devastation is a form of power and freedom that

many West Siders do not possess. This power has cultivated in me the need to tell their stories, our stories.

This anthology is an attempt to explore the dreams and realities of people living on the West Side of Chicago. The stories collected here celebrate and question how we understand and live with change—how we seek to understand ourselves in a not-so-understandable and not-so-comfortable world.

These stories suggest that the West Side is a case study in how Americans have not yet solved deep-seated social issues of race and the distribution of wealth. It remains to be seen whether or not African-Americans and Latinos, the dominant populations on the West Side of Chicago, can overcome cultural differences to offset the debilitating effects of class and economic stratification.

By the force of each writer's vision and language, the reader is carried into the living rooms and kitchens where the real folk of the West Side go about the business of living. Here, in *West Side Stories*, is an attempt to present the everyday, the brutal, the glorious.

The voices of this anthology are redemptive. They ask us to reclaim common rituals, impulses and embedded memories of people as ways of helping one another to get to where we all want to go. We all go together or we don't go at all.

George Bailey

Aaron Freeman

ACOUSTIC CATHOLICISM

My family converted to Roman Catholicism during its "Acoustic guitar period," in the mid-1960s, right after Vatican II convinced everybody that were Jesus alive today he'd have joined the cast of "Hair."

Though raised a Baptist, my mother was the first in the family to switch heavenly channels and has always been our most zealous Catholic. The two things that primarily attracted her and her circle of friends to the church were its social activism and its schools. They considered the archdiocesan educational system essential to making sure the "three Rs" their kids learned were not robbery, rioting and recidivism. That John Kennedy was Catholic made her feel better about both the religion and the candidate. I always had a sneaking suspicion my mother was also strongly attracted to Roman collars as a fashion statement. At that time, Nehru collars were tres in. But reason number one for her conversion was that Catholics were the white people most actively opposed to Mayor Richard J. Daley, which was all it took to make them her favorite white people on earth.

The first admitted Catholics I recall meeting were neither priests nor nuns. They were protoPriests, seminarians studying at Mundelein College. They were wholesome, well-scrubbed and almost without exception from the western suburbs. Maybe out that way they escaped the lake-effect bigotry. For a time, Catholic seminarians seemed determined to gang-convert our neighborhood. Suddenly they were everywhere. A huge pitcher of milk poured into the coffee pot of our "hood." Seminarians were shooting hoops with the cats in the project, preaching the gospel to children on weekends, helping paint signs for protests against then-School Superintendent Benjamin C. Willis, and strumming endless choruses of "Kumbaya My Lord" on the acoustic guitars they all carried, slung on their backs like musical AK-47s.

Our seminarians came every Saturday morning. Frank and Marty, I think their names were. They were big, strapping, USDA-approved white boys. Guys whose parents had clearly fed them much corn. It was the most significant cross-cultural experience of my childhood. They were not only teachers and ambassadors from distant exotic lands with wild, romantic names like "LaGrange" and "Elmhurst," but they were physical giants, to boot. Marty was at least a mile tall though he only admitted to six foot, seven inches.

They were there to prepare us for the jump into Catholispace. But as children of six or seven years, my sister Veronica and I had no appreciation of the conversion of Constantine, the doctrine of papal infallibility or the significance of celibacy. To us, being a Catholic meant new books to read, going to see Sean Connery as James Bond in *Thunderball*, and begging Frank and Marty to please not strum "Kumbaya My Lord" on that out-of-tune guitar anymore. Nonetheless, we were so fascinated by these gargantuan strangers that we'd have joined the Klan had Marty and Frank recommended it.

My memory of the conversion process is hazy, but they must have drilled us in the Baltimore Catechism. I can clearly recall that at various epochs of my life I have concocted new answers to the question, "Why did God make us?" These days my answer has something to do with multinational corporations and Macintosh computers. I am also reasonably certain we studied the Bible. And they apparently taught us well, because years later, in Catholic high school, I often found myself knowing just where in the Bible to look to find stuff to disagree with.

Had it not been for ten o'clock Sunday mass at St. Jarlath Church, named for a sixth-century Irish priest and now a secular vacant lot, I might never have known anything about Judaism. Don't get me wrong. I got no Judaic info in church. We were always taught that God was Jewish, but it was never explained or even implied that there was a culture, an ideology or, God forbid, a competing religion accompanying the fact. No, I was exposed to Judaism because as Veronica and I dressed for mass every Sunday morning we watched "The Magic Door" on Channel Two. We loved Tiny Tov and his acorn house and all his little puppet pals. Some Sundays we'd have such a good time hearing tales of Jehovah that we had to be physically dragged away to the house of Y'shua and even then we'd bop into the presence of the blessed virgin singing "Dradle, dradle, dradle, I made it out of clay. . ."

Catholics are still active on the near west side, though seminarians are no longer out in force. I guess today's western suburbanites figure it's pointless to help the poor since their parents did it back then, yet the poor still exist. Frank and Marty have been succeeded by four Mother Teresa nuns who, while not twenty-foot pituitary giants, are amazing characters.

When they first arrived at St. Malachy's, a reporter asked one of them, "There are only four of you. How can you minister to the twenty-thousand people of this parish?"

To which she replied, "That's nothing. When sister Jo and I were first in Mexico City, there were two of us for six million."

"What did you do?"

"I took three million and sister Jo took three million."

And the best thing is there's not a guitar player in the bunch.

HOME MOVIES

July. July so hot whole families escape the prison of their apartments to sleep in Grant Park near the lake. Whole families asleep, defenseless, out on the grass, in the open, and nobody afraid. It is 1935. Lindbergh is my mother's hero because he did what he said he would do. I stand on the front porch of our apartment and lean against the window, looking into the living room. I see my family sweating—my father, in an undershirt and wrinkled work pants; my mother, in a flowered housedress without the belt. I am seven years old and wearing puckered underpants. My sister, ten, has to wear a halter top with her puckered underpants. She is angry because I can go bare from the waist up.

We can't drive to Grant Park to sleep. We don't have a car. I put my mouth close to the window and say, very loud, "Use the Dodge!" They can't hear me, of course. Then I remember: We didn't buy the Dodge until 1945. With money my mother will earn during the war working in a defense plant—money for a new car, money for the bank account that will swell and then shrink when I go away to college. I want to wish the Dodge into our 1935 lives, but I don't know how. I want to offer them my 1975 Chevy sitting in my driveway now. There is no way to reach them.

Hot is hottest of all for families who live on the top floor, under flat roofs. In apartments with tiny windows that decide not to open that day. Louis sleeps in the smallest room under the flat roof in 1935. Only three miles from my seven-year-old life. I cross streets and backyards and alleys to watch him sleep. I want to invite him to sleep on our front porch, invite his whole family. But he doesn't know me then. We won't marry for 17 years. We may pass on the street, sit in the same movie theater on Saturday afternoons, run in the same gravel park, swim in the same public pool. Or we may not. Nothing would signal to either of us if we should brush past one another. He is 12, handsome. I am still in puckered underpants.

I stand outside his bedroom window, listen to him sleep, restless, twitching in his cocoon of damp sheets. His alarm rings. He wakes up slowly. He still does. He takes his clothes from a hook next to the bed, and goes into the next room. "Make your bed!" I call to him through the window. He still doesn't.

My father-in-law gets up one morning the winter I am ten and tells his wife he has an itch that must be scratched in California. He doesn't have a job and the Depression is less depressing in California in the sunshine, with oranges asking to be picked and mountains instead of streetcar tracks. She says, "Go. I'm staying. Me and the children."

He goes. Alone, without money or much language. He packs a cardboard suitcase and walks to the streetcar before it is light so he will not have to say good-bye to his children. He waits at the corner stop. Not far away, I am asleep in my ten-year-old body. I watch him in the weak circle of light from the streetlamp: a not-young, not-old man who has already forgotten what it is he will never have. "Don't go," I say, "You'll be sorry." He ignores me. "How can the children eat if you leave them? Louis wants to be a lawyer. How will that work out without a father?" He isn't listening. He looks past my face and into faces of people he hasn't met yet.

I try one last time. "You won't know your grandchildren if you go away." He will never know me anyhow. I will see him only once more, in his coffin. I will be carrying my first child. I am told that a pregnant woman must not look into an open coffin. It means bad luck. I look anyway, or how will I have a face to put to the memory of a man who is part of my husband, my children?

He knows he doesn't have to answer me. He gets on the red streetcar and rides alone to the Greyhound station downtown, where he waits five hours for the next bus west.

There is a postcard from California with a picture on it of Santa Claus, sweating in the sun, in front of Graumann's Chinese Theatre. And another card, and then nothing for a long time. My mother-in-law takes in boarders to pay the rent. Louis moves out of his room and sleeps in a double bed with his two brothers. After school he delivers meat for the kosher butcher. He brings brisket and chickens wrapped in waxy brown paper to our back door. I love watching him, serious, patient, while my mother searches for exactly the right change in her black leather purse with the torn lining. He takes two pink-and-crystal aggies out of his pocket, closes one eye and turns them very slowly until they catch the sun. I see why I will love him.

This is the year I have whooping cough. I hear him at the back door and try to hold my breath so I won't cough until he has gone. I can't, and a cough sputters out. He shows no sign he has heard. It is a sound that has no connection to his life. Twenty years later he and I will take turns moving out of our sleep, summoned down cold halls by other childhood coughs.

This is the spring I sit up nights choking. The doctor says that the clean air from the lake will help me sleep. My father, exhausted from his rounds as a milkman, naps for a half hour after his supper, then drives me to the lake in his brother's new blue Essex. We sit in the car alone together on the deserted pier, through the long city night. We can hear the water. I sleep sitting up. My father plays the radio softly to stay awake so he can watch me. In the morning, before six o'clock, we go to Thompson's Cafeteria on Michigan Avenue for breakfast. We are the first customers. I bite into my toast and cough. I cough so hard I spit my juice and my milk all over the floor. My father takes a blue handkerchief out of his pocket and wipes my face. I am crying because the man and woman in white uniforms standing behind the counter are watching. My father kisses my cheek and asks the manager for a broom and dustpan.

My mother-in-law is wheeling a baby buggy down the summer street. It is 1940. I watch her from the corner. "You don't have a baby anymore," I say to her when she passes. I follow just behind her on her right so I can see into the buggy. I see a pink blanket and the tip of a baby's bonnet. I can't see the baby's face. She is walking faster now and looks over her shoulder with frightened eyes. She stops in front of a grocery store, opens the door, pushes the buggy through. A man comes out from behind the counter and wipes his hands on his dirty apron. He steps to the door and looks out, first in one direction and then in the other. He tells her that nobody is following her.

My mother-in-law folds the pink blanket back and lifts something very heavy out of the buggy. It is a half-gallon crockery jug. The man takes it from her and hands her a one-dollar bill. He puts the jug on the floor behind the counter. She looks at the dollar bill for a moment, folds it in half and puts it inside the front of her cotton dress. Then she leaves quickly, almost bumping my leg with the wheel of the buggy. I wait and watch the grocer pour a brown liquid from the jug into a paper cup, then drink. He smacks his lips and looks satisfied. Schnapps!

Years later, sitting over Passover wine at Seders—long after she is dead—her children will tell my children how she made whisky in a washtub and sold it to buy them food. I have questions to ask this woman in whose womb Louis gathered the strength to become who he is. But when I am young, there is never enough time; when I am old enough to understand how important it is to ask her, she has gone, taking her answers with her.

We can go to the lake now any time we want to. We can walk there, we live so close. Summer mornings, when the girls are home, I fix sandwiches and we walk together through streets shaded by oaks and dogwood. It's an easy walk, a beautiful one. Usually the streets are empty on these hot summer days. And quiet. It's a quiet that leaves room for me to hear other street sounds, sounds happening very far away, in the city, where the lake washes past concrete sidewalks and thirsty lawns. I hear a fire siren; a stick banging against a garbage can; hot, cranky children, cramped in their sticky bodies; women arguing on front stoops. Then it's quiet again. And that's when I can hear behind me the lagging footsteps of a little girl. When I turn around very quickly, sometimes I can see her in her puckered underpants.

Tony Del Valle

VOICES

The ride from the airport was unbearable for Helena. Floating on the hum of wheels over chilled, glistening asphalt, she felt sick with happiness. She was tickled by the pointed edges and tones of the conversation going on in the front seat of the cab. Her dad sounded so suave and confident, and the cab driver kept referring to him as Mr. Palacios. Her mom had been transformed into another woman who laughed giddily at dad's stories. They all burst into laughter as José finished telling Sarah a story about a "Puertorro" in a restaurant who had to cackle and flap his arms like wings to make the waiter understand his order.

"Yes, life can be very tough in Chicago, Señora Palacios," said the cab driver, speaking this time to Helena's mother, "but if you work hard, take care of your family and lead a clean life, you can live just like the rich folks. And it wouldn't hurt if you swallow your pride and try to pick up a little English along the way."

Helena looked out through the mist on the windows, fascinated by yellow beams of light from other cars sweeping through the inside of the cab. She took in the smell of clean car and gasoline and cuddled up against the woolly texture of Benjamin's and Camil's winter coats. She wore shiny black shoes, new white socks that folded to reveal little purple flowers and still smaller leaves.

Helena couldn't wait for the cab to stop in front of their new home. When they got off the expressway she could not believe what was actually happening. She feared that this could be a hoax. She feared that someone would stop the cab and say, "Okay, let's turn this whole thing back; why should these kids be allowed to escape from where they belong. Toss them back across the ocean." Stinging images flickered across Helena's closed eyelids.

"They belong back there without their dad; with buzzards, with angry grandfathers with straw huts and bad 'presagios.'"

Perhaps that was an impostor sitting in front, pretending to be her dad. Any minute, the cab driver would turn around and say, "Ha-ha, fooled you!" She began thinking this was a fantasy, that someone was letting them live, to relive their past desperation of getting out of that life on Buzzard Hill. Maybe, she thought, they had died, and this was the end of life—to travel perpetually in this car, living her dearest fantasy before arriving in heaven. She began to feel sleepy and the bad thoughts drifted out of her mind like remnants of a bad dream. She decided to make sure to keep her eyes closed until the cab approached her new home, and open them at the last minute when it was time to get out.

And tomorrow, Helena wanted to run out into the streets to see in the flesh the people she had seen in American magazines; gas stations, people in boats, picnics; blond, blue-eyed babies in strollers. She wanted to see the many different kinds of cars, bridges, buildings, parks. Were there really such things as parks with green wooden benches and glass lamps? Were there merry-go-rounds with coy, prancing horses of many colors as she had seen in books—trains with sleeping compartments and dining rooms? Buses? Supermarkets, shopping carts?

Women who wore lipstick and spoke English? Elevators? A lake? Zoos? Impossible. That stuff was really make-believe, created by the people who wrote her school books.

Her father turned on the car radio and glanced at the back seat. A song about "Big Big John" poured out of the cab walls in a deep clean voice.

That was followed by another song sung by a lady, who, judging by her voice, must have been incredibly beautiful.

> . . . and the love that I found,
> ever since you've been around
> you have put me at the top of the world.

Helena smiled and allowed herself to slide gently into sleep. Benjamin, Camil and Julian were all deep into their own thoughts, staring out the windows. Camil and Julian felt too scared to look at each other in the eyes. They didn't want the others to detect the astonishment, in their faces, to the answer of what had seemed, for the last three or four years endless, hopeless prayers.

In her dream, everything is straight lines, geometric shapes. Helena gets the feeling that this is all a set-up, that behind a few houses there is wilderness like the one on Buzzard Hill. She runs away from this facade like a western town in the movies. Her teacher had warned her about the facades created by Hollywood. She runs a long way thinking that eventually she will begin to see green valleys, trees, and mountains in the distance, but the concrete and brick never ends. There is the smell of hot concrete, green, lemon-yellow and pink peeling paint on the sides of buildings smelling like candy. Sidewalks, corners, angular rooftops, stretch into infinity and above them the sky, a dirty blue. Then she is back at the airport. People bark. They pretend to be speaking English. And sometimes, when they think they are out of earshot of Spanish speakers, they speak in Spanish and become friendly; they abandon the farce of being cold and indifferent and oh-so-cosmopolitan and phony with each other.

They arrived at 1915 W. Concord Street. Helena waited in her seat, holding out, but Camil was thinking the same thoughts and she sat low, chin on her chest, her shoulders into the crevice of the back seat. Helena didn't want anyone to see her reactions. She wanted to see everyone else's reaction. She looked to her left. Through the car window the darkness above the buildings was beginning to thin into navy blue. "This is a different sky," she thought. "This is the same sky, but a different world." When she turned to look at Camil, she found an empty space on the seat. She grabbed the brown paper bag stuffed down at her feet and shifted over to the open door. There she met her mother's hand, on its way to get her. The morning was foggy and cold.

There were scruffy shrubs in front of the sooty brick building. José led the way through the entrance, a two-step front porch with two brick columns and spider webs under its awning.

"It's the third floor," Helena heard her father say. When they reached the second floor, José asked Sarah and the children to go on ahead and returned to pay the cabby. Helena, Camil, Benjamin and Julian raced for the top landing talking and laughing. Helena could hardly contain her bladder. They hadn't realized they were talking loud until they heard José shush them from downstairs. Benjamin, who felt he had been swimming in an ocean of love and indulgence since he stepped off the plane, now felt his elation wane. José's shush made him stop five steps before the final landing and straighten up. He felt his stomach get hard and cold. He extended his right arm out and held Julian back at his stomach. "Shush!" he said, and continued climbing in an extra quiet tippy-toe.

When they arrived at the top landing they saw two doors, dark brown. They didn't know which one was the entrance to their new home. Julian got on all fours at the right door trying to peek inside the apartment through the keyhole. He started sneezing and got up realizing he wouldn't be able to see anything. Camil saw the cabbie arrive on the third floor landing before José and Sarah, out of breath, carrying two sagging suitcases. They had split open in the plane and clothes had dropped out on the conveyor belt like overstuffed sandwiches. José had quickly procured some tape and string and, in the middle of a pushing and shoving crowd, wrapped the suitcases as tight as he could. He had told Sarah in his last letter not to worry about having money to buy enough suitcases. The important thing, he wrote, was that they get here even if only with the clothes they had on. The plane ride was only going to last a few hours and if people noticed and criticized, the hell with them. Camil got teary-eyed when she read those lines in which her father put things in such a way that not even the most shameful circumstances could make her feel completely desperate and abandoned.

The cab driver went back downstairs. Camil heard the cab driver ask José and Sarah if they needed any more help, and then heard them chit-chat without any sense of urgency. José carried tomato sauce boxes under each arm. The boxes, wrapped tight with tape and string, were now doing duty as luggage. Sarah carried a flower-print pillow case filled with underwear, José's letters, crucifixes, framed icons of Mother Mary and Judas Tadeo, and vomit-laden towels. She wrapped the top part of the bag into a knot around her hand, let it hang at her side. She heard the rosary beads and other loose objects rattle against the cracked glass of one of the icons as she took each step.

When her mother and father turned on the landing to climb the last set of steps, Camil noticed in the milky light that they were both smiling, chuckling about something one of them said. Then they stood, finally, in the bright light from the skylight above the top landing. Benjamin noticed that his dad's coat was not new. It was immaculately clean, but there were shiny wear spots under the cuffs. When José finally opened the door, all the children except Julian ran into the dark apartment. Camil and Helena walked toward the kitchen, stopping briefly at the door of the middle bedroom. They wanted the lights on right away. Benjamin walked to the other side of the apartment toward the small bedroom near the living room. He peeked quickly into the bedroom, looked out the front windows down into the street and then turned to join his sisters. Julian looked up at José's face and then hung on to José's pant leg, feeling odd at seeking protection from someone who was his father and yet felt like a stranger. He switched over to Sarah's leg and José set the suitcases and boxes in the inside hallway, watching the children and Sarah's reactions.

Helena came back into the living room and confirmed things she had barely distinguished in the living room as they rushed in. She saw a sofa—an actual sofa, and across from it a smaller one and on the corners two sofa chairs. They looked better than Tia Romana's. Helena walked around in the semi-darkness, sitting on each one. Then she walked to the middle and got on one knee to touch the middle table, carefully, the way a blind person touches everything. It was smooth and cold, its sides decorated with grooves and small half-spheres. "I can't believe this is ours," she thought. "I can't believe this is mine: mine! mine! mine!" The middle table stood at the center of a beige rug which extended to within a few inches from the sideboards. All the wood, including the floorboards, was dark and covered with heavy, uneven varnish. The walls were covered with old, mint-green wallpaper with prints of tiny cinnamon and white flowers and green leaves on boughs. Camil, who had been bouncing on the bed in the middle room still holding the brown bag she had brought on the plane, came back into the living room and repeated Helena's steps around the living room seats.

After asking José for directions, Sarah walked Julian to the washroom. Benjamin followed close behind.

"How does this work?" asked Sarah in the dark, looking for the string José said would be there for the light. Benjamin walked in ahead of her and with one sweep of his arms in the dark, found the string and pulled it. A weak, yellow light came on in the ceiling. Accidental brush strokes darkened the bulb which hung nested in a sloppily painted light green cone. Benjamin walked to the toilet while unzipping. He examined the apparatus from a distance. An actual toilet, slightly rust-stained on the inside, sweating on the square porcelain base that was one and the same with the bowl on top. By the time he had finished urinating, Sarah had helped Julian take out his penis and he joined his brother at the toilet. Sarah stood behind them, both coats in front of her, draped over her arms. At that moment she loved seeing her sons standing side by side, she loved her life, she loved this man who could be such a loving provider. She wanted to tell him how she felt, but didn't know how to say it and not sound so sentimental that it ended up sounding insincere. She shifted her weight to her left foot. Buying high heel shoes to come to the States sounded like a good idea when she talked it over with Godmother Victoria. But all the walking at the airport in Puerto Rico, waiting in line on the hot tarmac to reach the stairs to the plane only to wait there again, and then the walk through the airport here! She couldn't wait to get her toes out of the pencil point of the shoes and out into the open, let them expand to their normal size and keep on expanding if they wanted. She knew how good it would feel. Benjamin finished urinating and looked at the bathtub. The left faucet knob, shaped like a little cartwheel, dripped incessantly, wearing down the porcelain in a pear-shaped black stain. The tub was like a big white canoe sitting on four dog paws. He imagined himself submerged in wonderfully warm crystalline water surrounded by this smooth, white cocoon. Ben pounded the tub with his right hand and listened to the dull ring.

Then he heard the toilet flush and turned quickly to watch. Julian stood watching and listening with him while Sarah left the washroom to go find José. "Now remember, Julian," said Benjamin, feigning all seriousness. "You're not supposed to drink from this. If you want water, you go to the kitchen and get it from the faucet. Like this one." He pointed to the spigot on the face bowl. He remembered the airport bathroom where they had encountered a strange row of porcelain receptacles gurgling, and pipes vibrating with internal effervescence. When he saw a man come away from one of the receptacles closing his zipper, he had figured it out: one was supposed to urinate in them. He did as the others did and suddenly remembered Julian. When he looked down the row of urinals, there he was, sucking water from the stream running down the back wall of the urinal.

Sarah and José called from the bedroom and asked them to take their clothes off, and put on their pajamas—pajamas?—and try to get some sleep. After a few minutes of showing off their pajamas to each other they got in bed.

José came in the dark and sat on the edge of Julian and Benjamin's bed. He ran his fingers through Julian's hair. "My son. I thought sometimes I would never see you again." Then he noticed Benjamin getting close to his hand and ran his fingers through Benjamin's hair. "Dad?" asked Benjamin. "When is it going to snow?" José chuckled. "Oh Ben, it'll snow soon enough . . . soon enough." Winters gave him horrible nose bleeds, and here was Ben, asking when will it snow.

"But dad, why isn't there snow out there? It's already cold." Julian set the side of his face on the

back of José's hand. Benjamin sighed in mock
exasperation. "Julian, it has to get real real cold
before it snows."

"But it's getting real cold already, right, dad?"

"'Se esta poniendo frio si, ay bendito!'" said José
in a voice and tone not his own. The boys laughed at
José's strange outburst, and the girls, who had been
listening in the next room giggled hysterically loud
enough to let them know they'd been listening. José
chuckled too, then said, "There is this man who lives
around here; well actually, he sleeps in a gangway
around here, who is always saying that out loud. 'Se
esta poniendo frio si, ay bendito!'" The children
laughed again. "OK, God bless you, now go to
sleep." He tucked them in and left to tuck the girls
in. Then Julian heard Helena ask for water so he
asked for water as well. José made several trips to
the kitchen and soon all four children had a drink of
water. Benjamin squeezed himself into the warmth of
his body and his blanket. He smelled the clean
pillow, felt the strangeness of his own body under
crisp clean blankets covering him head to toe and
then some. His own pillow! He could not believe he
was here. He felt afraid something wrong would
happen—a fire! Then he realized he was thinking
silly thoughts, silly thoughts that might actually bring
about what he feared. He heard mom and dad
whispering and murmuring in the bedroom down the
hall and felt deeply that this was where they
belonged: together. As long as they remained
together everything was safe, there was nothing to be
feared, anything was possible. School would be a
breeze.

Benjamin was startled awake after sleeping, he
didn't know for how long. He heard the floor

creaking under barefoot steps and then saw the dark contour of a figure walking across the open door of his bedroom toward the kitchen. His mind raced, topsy-turvy. He got up and walked carefully to the bedroom door and peered into the darkness of the kitchen. He saw a shadow, this time created by light bent across the ceiling and the right wall of the kitchen. He tiptoed closer and saw it was Camil in her floor-length sleeping gown standing in front of the open refrigerator filling a glass with milk. He snuck up on her and surprised her. She let out a low squeal and then shushed him. But Benjamin was not paying attention to her. His eyes were wide and full of all the things he saw in the refrigerator, like something out of a school book: a gallon of milk, butter sticks, eggs, Coca-Colas! He went to open the freezer, but Camil stopped him. Then she helped him open it. They saw a doughnut of ice and bloodstained frost, its hole stuffed with what looked like chicken and pork chops. Incredible. Ben bent slightly and looked into the lower shelves.

"Look! Jelly! And, and peanut butter!"

"Shhh!" Camil looked over her shoulder into the dark hallway. Benjamin hunched his shoulders at her reproof and brought his hand toward his pursed lips as if to prevent more exclamations from escaping. Camil filled the glass again and turned to see Benjamin reaching for a glass from the sink next to the refrigerator. She pulled back his arm by the wrist and shoved her full glass into Benjamin's chest. She was afraid that if they drank too much milk, Dad would notice it in the morning and give them their first punishment in the United States. As Benjamin drank, he noticed that Camil had a milk moustache and started laughing into his milk. Camil ran the

back of her hand over her mouth and when she
noticed the moisture she had wiped she also laughed.
When Benjamin was done, Camil rinsed the glass.
She threw her arm over Benjamin's shoulder and they
walked down the dark hallway to their bedrooms.
"Se esta poniendo frio si, ay bendito!"

Helena blinked and wondered if she had been
dreaming she had heard the alley man. She looked at
the ceiling and didn't recognize it. There were
supposed to be wooden rafters and corrugated zinc
planks up there. Then she remembered: she was now
in the United States, the whole family was in the
United States living with Dad. She tried to fall back
asleep and deal with the shock later.

"Se esta poniendo frio si, ay bendito!" she heard
the man say, when she had almost fallen asleep
again.

She threw the cover off and walked to the window
to try and catch a glimpse of the alley man. Then
Julian and Benjamin came quietly into the room. The
four looked at each other for a moment; then,
without saying a word, burst into an uncontrollable
laughter that brought tears to their eyes. When it
stopped, they huddled together under the blankets
and waited for the clarity of daylight.

CALIFORNIA

Cal Weathers liked Oleg Lum because of his name. Nothing else recommended the earnest Russian who was now shucking oysters next to Cal at The Shell. Since Oleg's arrival, no one joked about Cal's name being California or asked him about the weather on the coast. Instead, they said, "Oh, Leg!" when the worst kitchen jobs had to be performed. Just seeing Oleg display his incompetence boldly as a badge made Cal smile.

"What is funny?" Oleg would ask.

"You, man," Cal would answer, shaking his head and letting another gritty oyster slither onto the shaved ice.

When they had finished their early morning shifts as salad preparers, Cal and Oleg would wash their hands with Boraxo and take their lunches to the card table covered with red oilcloth where the help ate, that is, if Mr. Perke wasn't around. Sometimes the table would be cluttered with week-old guest checks that Mr. Perke totalled on an adding machine that trailed a pink row of numbers onto the floor.

"They're giving the place away!" he'd wail mostly to himself and then add, "Damn bitches!" to include any employee who had the potential to add a check incorrectly.

"Is good food," Oleg commented over his plate of perch and grayish peas.

"Is beginning to stink," Cal mimicked.

At first Oleg hadn't been sure he liked Cal. Cal looked menacing to Oleg, who'd seen few black

people before he left Russia. He remembered one
Ethiopian student he'd known in Moscow, how
fascinated he'd been to observe the cold Russian air
circulating through Tesfaye's lungs and out of his
thin, fine nose. There was nothing about Cal that
Oleg would call refined. His jaw had been broken
and was jerryrigged to the rest of his face. Oleg
wondered what held it there. Cal's hands also
frightened him, seeming to be too large to connect at
his thin wrists. The wrists led to bulging forearms.
His arms seemed wasted at the restaurant. Oleg
imagined them better serving an iron worker.

"You were once blacksmith?" he'd asked Cal
several weeks ago.

Cal had looked puzzled before telling Oleg that
he'd never belonged to a street gang.

Sometimes their lunch hours would be taken up by
Cal's political tirades. He'd always talk so low that
Mr. Perke could only imagine what he was telling
Oleg. Oleg would lean across the table to catch Cal's
words.

"See President Peckerwood last night on TV?"

"You mean U. S. President?"

"President Peckerwood. Lives in the Bird House."

"I saw news of president's trip to Rome."

"Peckerwood's always smiling like he's smelling
sweet shit. His wife's real hot. He divorced his first
wife because she got fat. Republicans like that."

"Is true?"

"I read all about it. Don't you read books, Oleg?
How do you imagine you're going to make your way
in Peckerland?"

Oleg reached for more tartar sauce and stared at
his plate. He was afraid when Cal spoke this way.

"Is wonderful country where you can call president bad language."

"Ain't it great? We elect rat brains like him so we can exercise our right to complain. Have you read up on it? I was just going to use mine to tell Perke that I want Saturday off. My grandma died again."

"I am sorry to hear. She was ill?"

"She was dead. Been dead since last time I wanted Saturday off. If Perke had a memory, waitresses wouldn't steal him blind. You watch. I'll ask and he'll say 'fine.'"

Everyday when Oleg left work he used a different phone booth for his call to Claire. So far he'd tried booths on Grand between Wabash and Wells. Today he'd taken the El all the way home to try a new one.

"Today it's weaving. She's on a real self-improvement kick," Carrie explained. "Mom's even taking a class in making Christmas cookies, and we're Jewish! I'll tell her you called, Oleg."

"Is she unhappy that I call?"

"No, she smiles, and she still thinks about Bop, too. You know, they never found the baby's parents. Mom said they put him in a foster home."

"And I can maybe visit?"

"I asked Mom that. She doesn't know if you can even though you found him. You'll have to call the police. They might know."

"Let's get ripped," Cal said to Oleg after he finished Thursday's shift.

"I do not understand."

"What do you Russkies understand? Do you understand vodka?"

"Is great painkiller," Oleg said quietly. He was afraid that Mr. Perke planted spies among the kitchen help and that he was in imminent danger of losing his job for talking about sordid topics.

"Get ripped. Drink vodka." He raised an imaginary shot glass to his lips. When he thought Oleg didn't understand, he became monosyllabic.

"Drinking is sometimes good," Oleg continued, "but today I am busy. I hear that baby I found at beach and know better than any American is not owned by parents. He is in special home for orphan babies. I would own this baby or Claire, who is beautiful, but can have no more babies."

"C'mon, Oleg. We can have drinks and then I'll help you get this baby. Once my old lady moved out on me with my three babies. Lamont's the oldest. He looks like me before I got my new chin. Fred's in the middle. He's mean like his mamma. Baby Cal's just like me. He's only three. It's not true you love yours all the same."

"You must be proud father. I was married to getting out of Russia, idea that owned me like wife. I work very hard, and now I am here. Can you tell me how I might own this baby?"

"C'mon, I'll buy you a few drinks next door. We'll watch a little TV."

"Is okay, Cal. I drink with you, and then maybe we find baby even today."

"It can happen that fast, Oleg. A baby can be lost or found in no time. Once this dude I know named Harold was staying at his old lady's. She had to go to work, so Harold says he'll watch the kid. Baby's no older than two. So Harold's been up all night. He's watching the baby. Then he hears, 'Wake up! You're under arrest!' Seems he fell asleep and the baby walked right out the front door. Two cops found him standing in front of Comiskey Park. So babies get lost fast."

"It happened for baby Bop at beach where drug-taking parents leave him. I am sorry to say that Claire called police and baby was taken away. I say to Claire, 'Keep smart baby!' but she is afraid."

"Who ain't?"

After toasting the recent improvement of American and Russian relations, President Peckerwood and his wife, Claire, Carrie, Bop, Lamont and Baby Cal, they started on toasts for improvement. Oleg wished that Cal's middle son would prove acceptable. Cal wished that Oleg would be reunited with Bop.

"People think that guys wanting babies are a little funny, Oleg. You know, there was a guy who dressed like a clown and killed boys."

Oleg looked indignant. "Is not my hope to be killing clown."

"People think the worst. For instance, the first day I saw you, I thought you'd be a real loser. People is prejudiced."

"I go to police and explain. I tell them baby is like stolen bicycle. If found and no owner, I can keep it."

"I'd just say you found a child and would like to know its whereabouts."

"Okay, we say that."

"We?"

"Cal and Oleg say that to officers."

"What good will that do? 'Who's he?' they'll ask. 'Your good thang?' No, you go alone and act real serious, like you're in a white people's church."

"Okay, I say, 'Police, I was finder of lost baby. I feed it and it sleeps in my house. Then I return it to you, and you give it to false parents.'"

"I'd be cool, Oleg. If you say things like *false*, they'll get all riled up, and you won't get a thing."

"Maybe I should wait for Claire, the woman who gives baby to police?"

"Sure, we'll have more drinks. Then Claire can go with you. Police can't resist mothers. Once when I was incarcerated, my mother came. Ten minutes later I was walking."

"You are then criminal?"

"Everyone's a criminal, Oleg. You just need a little time and less money, and you'll be one, too."

Oleg had seen the ring in a pawnshop on Devon Avenue. Pawnshops were sadder to him than anything else about America. No one could convince Oleg that possessions weren't loved. He remembered the transistor radio he'd bought on the black market in Moscow. It was shaped like a Coke bottle. For many years it had been his skyline. It wasn't the object itself but the owner's feelings for it. The sillier the object, the better. The more ostentatious, the better. The more one needed to sacrifice for it, the better. The more degrading its surroundings, the better it looked in contrast.

The ring was the perfect embodiment of useless pleasure. The thought of wearing it while shucking oysters in the smoky restaurant delighted him. He'd waited a month for the owner to repossess it, but it was still in the window on the day he'd set for the purchase.

He hoped the ring would purge his current mood, the darkest he'd felt since he left Russia. The desolation of September with the beaches closing, Carrie back in school, Claire busy with her life, and his new job at The Shell left him wondering if he'd left Russia at all, or if Russia was a malady one had for a lifetime, a chill from the tundra producing visions of imminent doom. Even the letters he wrote to the newspaper's *Personal View* column were colored by his new bitterness, a word he thought he'd left behind him.

Sometimes Carrie's normal ten-year-old nonchalance annoyed him. The world had no time for ambivalence, he wanted to tell her. Lots of people needed to be warned to change their lives. He'd make his way about the city dispensing wisdom. Mr. Kaplan, for instance, who had fired Oleg from his last job in security for not calling the police, should be apprised of their nature. Nothing was worse than official thugs, not even the thugs that remove cars from parking lots after disconnecting the finely tuned alarm systems. They were in business for themselves. They were committed personally to Free Enterprise. They risked their lives for shiny fenders, leather seats and metallic blue paint. The police risked their lives for a paycheck. They interfered with the individual's religious urge toward ownership. It was hard to understand how a free country could tolerate such purveyors of injustice.

When Oleg first shopped in American groceries, he wondered why his fellow Russians were always buying the brashest colors of toilet paper. Then he remembered the toilet paper queues in Russia. If there were orange toilet paper in America or red with sequins, all the better. It was beautiful to waste beauty. He began winking at old women, so spare in the rest of their shopping. Their carts contained generic cans, cream cheese, and the beautiful toilet paper, usually in shocking pink. Oleg made a mental note to write a new *Personal View* column. Toilet paper might well be the subject.

Upon entering the pawnshop, he took an immediate dislike to the salesman. Why didn't Americans, who were charged with the most awesome responsibilities, show any enthusiasm for their jobs? He'd give anything to buy back loved items from desperate people and sell them to ardent new owners. People didn't understand the drama or pathos of their own lives. Once he'd seen a man sitting on a gray couch on the sidewalk amid his belongings. When a neighbor had explained to Oleg that the man had been evicted, he was amazed by the man's calm reserve. Why didn't people beat their breasts in indignation?

"May I help you?" the young man was repeating. He was perhaps twenty-five and had thinning hair. His face looked refined and his eyes were small and alert. He was reading a newspaper even as he asked Oleg if he needed assistance.

"I am interested, please, in the diamond for the hand."

"The Mason's ring? It's a good one, a real one." The young man theatrically displayed a jewel-inspecting device that reminded Oleg of a periscope.

"Please, I can use?" Oleg put the instrument to his eye and enjoyed the prismatic effect of the stone.

"I'll give it to you for four-fifty. You can pay it all at once or put down a hundred."

"Please, I can try it on?"

"Sorry, sir. I can let you try on another ring in the same size, but our diamond jewelry isn't available for wearing before purchase. It's part of our new loss prevention plan."

Maybe all the cameras in the window were burglary devices and the mindless television screens contained video recording equipment. Maybe the man behind the barred window had a gun trained on Oleg. His left temple throbbed in response to the image.

The man handed Oleg a discolored silver circle the same size as the ring. It fit him snugly. "Now I am married to loss prevention."

"You can put $100 down and sign a contract to pay the rest on time. We offer 21% financing, which is very good these days, and we have a thirty-day return policy. If you decide to return the ring within that period of time, you can have your money back minus a $20 handling fee. Here are the papers explaining this method of payment."

"And if the ring is wanted by old owner?"

"Once the ring is sold, it's yours. Previous ownership is invalidated. You know, *no backsies*, as we used to say in marbles."

"Is this U. S. law?"

"I don't imagine that I represent the view of the whole government. Pawnshop law is different."

"I will pay $100 and sign mortgage document."

Oleg signed the papers in triplicate, bought an old Brownie camera for Carrie and a digital alarm for Claire. As he carried the items out of the store, he couldn't take his eyes off his hand.

In the few hours that remained before dinner, he'd work on a *Personal View* article for the paper.

Dear Personal View:

Pawnshop law is very good American practice according to Oleg Lum, who purchased diamond from tragic Mason who cannot keep what he loves. I think too that pawnshop law would be valuable justice tool in missing child cases. Parents get a certain time to claim lost child. If child is unclaimed, than any person who has $450, the price of beautiful Mason ring, can own child. There is no need for police in Pawnshop Adoption Plan. It can be business deal involving no backsies. One could sign contract from listless pawnshop man and baby would benefit from new owner who loves his possession. If today I could buy baby I find at beach for all the money I own ($5,245), I would sign and pay interest forever.

Thank you,

Oleg Lum

At nine o'clock they decided to begin dinner even though Cal hadn't arrived.

"Cal is casual man," Oleg assured Carrie and Claire, who were more hungry than interested in the personality of Oleg's new friend. "He is sometimes late for work and sometimes leaves early. He is sometimes sober and sometimes not. Maybe today is not sober day, or one of his three handsome sons has trouble and Cal must play parole officer."

"Are his kids in prison?" Carrie asked.

"No, is little joke I make about school for you, Carrie."

"Oleg, I bought some tickets for a flute concert. Would you like to join us on Sunday?"

"I am delighted to go to concert and to wear my new ring from beautiful land of dreams, pawnshop."

"You got our things at a pawnshop? Aren't things at pawnshops stolen?"

"Is not stolen but sacrificed. The new owners buy and love more than old ones."

"I think he's talking about Bop," Carrie said, digging her fork into her mashed potatoes.

"Did I tell you, Oleg, that the DCFS found him some foster parents?" Claire sounded nervous. She knew Oleg wouldn't be disarmed by qualifiers such as *nice* or *responsible*. "And do you know what his real name is, Oleg? Your lost baby is Gary."

"Is still Bop. Is lost without me."

Claire clanked her wine glass into her plate. Carrie jumped to attention.

"Cal says police can get back child. That we go to police together. Once when Cal needed release, his mother came and won his freedom."

"This guy's a criminal?" Carrie shrieked joyously. "What did he do?"

"Little Carrie, everyone in America is criminal if he has less money and little time. I have much money to spend on regaining little Bop."

"You'll need a lawyer, not the police, Oleg. And there's little chance that a bachelor so new to this country would qualify to adopt a child."

"There are many babies needing homes. I am good shopper. I want the real baby, Bop."

The buzzer rang.

Oleg had never seen Cal so dressed up. He wore a mustard-colored leisure suit, black patent leather shoes, and a white shirt with a mustard, orange and brown brocade collar. Upon entering the apartment, he smiled broadly at Oleg and said to Claire, "For the lady of the house." He handed her a closed aluminum can that Oleg recognized from the restaurant as one of his plunders.

"Thank you!" Claire exclaimed.

"Oysters look like dead brains," Carrie added.

"Carrie, oysters are high in protein and considered very fancy."

"Oysters are love food," Cal added smiling at Oleg, Carrie and Claire. "Sorry I'm late, by the way."

"There's still plenty to eat."

Oleg was busy serving his friend the leftover food.

"Oleg tells me you're a good cook." Every time that Cal spoke, he shared a peripheral nod with Oleg. They were conspirators trained in Mr. Perke's kitchen to load their phrases with meaning.

"This is the first time we've had a black person to dinner," Carrie added. "I've read a lot about black people like Harriet Tubman."

"Carrie, what's the point? We know all kinds of people. Oleg's spoken of you so often that we feel as if we know you."

Oleg and Cal stood in front of Claire's building. Dinner had been a limited success. Most of the topics for conversation had been Carrie's and included river rats, Frederick Douglass, men who kill women with electric drills, and why adults lie to children. Outside the night was dark, and the moon seemed unremarkable.

"See the ring, Oleg?"

Oleg held his hand up to Cal's face. His eyes were filled with light. "Is it not lovely?"

"Beautiful, Oleg. You know, I'm going to one big card game tonight. I could really make a killing. I have on my new duds. You like my suit? What I need are some accessories. And you know what would make a fine accessory?" When Oleg didn't answer, Cal continued. "Your ring, Oleg. I'd give it back tomorrow."

"Is too valuable to me."

"I know, Oleg. I'll take care of it. Don't sweat."

"I cannot give away my property. Sorry, Cal, but ring is mine."

"I know it's yours, Oleg. I just want to flash it around for you. What good is it on your hand when you're fast asleep in bed?"

"Is my dream."

"Is just what my luck needs."

"I can say maybe okay but just for one night. You will write a note saying I can have backsies."

"Where do you get your English?"

"Man at pawnshop says 'backsies.'"

"You'll have the ring tomorrow. I'll give you a bonus if I do fine tonight."

"I can go to card game, Cal? You can wear my ring, but American card game is great event to me like World Series."

"You play stud?"

"No."

"Well, there's no spectating in this game. It's pretty rough."

Oleg handed Cal the ring and folded the note into his wallet. He waved good-bye.

The first day that Cal was out of work, Oleg assumed he'd had a late night playing cards. He told Mr. Perke he was certain that Cal would be back the next day. Mr. Perke didn't seem to believe him, but then again, Mr. Perke didn't believe anyone. Oleg didn't think that Cal had a phone, but he knew his address from the employee punch-in card.

The night before he'd dreamed that his ring had fallen into a sewer grate and that a large woman had retrieved it before he could protest. In his dream a policeman dressed in a white suit and shiny gray glasses had arrested the woman, handed Oleg his ring and asked if he was missing a baby, too.

Oysters were piling up on the shaved ice. His hands were speedier when Cal wasn't around. He began worrying that he was working too fast. He didn't want Mr. Perke to think he hadn't worked hard the other days. To slow himself down, he only had to think of Cal and his missing ring.

"Hey, Leg, stop with the oysters and get the soup crock ready," Perke called.

"Yes, I do."

"I don't care if you do or don't. Get the lousy soup in the crock."

Oleg had heard that the West Side once had great mansions. He remembered reading the descriptions in *Sister Carrie*. Here he was riding down the same street that Dreiser had described, West Jackson Boulevard. He saw a great many television repair stores and some large, mysterious warehouses. He wondered if nothing else happened on the West Side but TVs breaking down and needing treatment. He was happy that his own black and white set still worked. The antenna needed occasional adjusting, and he'd added a few pieces of tin foil for better reception, but that was to be expected.

2121 West Jackson was a red three-flat with gray trim. When he rang the bell, a dog began barking. He wondered if it was Cal's dog. Cal had never mentioned owning a pet, not even when Carrie had asked him directly at dinner.

"What do you want?" a woman was saying.

"Is Mr. Weathers home, please. I am friend from work."

"Mr. Weathers ain't never home. Not now. Not later. Mr. Weathers don't work, either. You sure you got the right person?"

"Cal Weathers. Father of three boys. Card player. Once incarcerated."

"Once plus about four. Cal will take what ain't his not matter whose it is. See my wedding ring?"

Oleg looked down at her empty hand.

"That's right. Ain't one there. Used to be, but Cal needed it back. Let's just say I wasn't too willing to give it to him. Did he take something from you, too? If he did, you understand I ain't responsible. I don't know why people go around trusting that man. He seems so friendly, don't he?"

A little boy came up to the door and looked peevishly at Oleg.

"You are Baby Cal?"

The boy wrapped himself around his mother's legs. "I call him Calvin. It means something to name a child. I ain't calling this one Cal. Bad luck."

"Please, but Cal is never here?"

"Oh, he tries sometimes, but it's always the same. Too much of everything but sense."

"I am sorry to be bothering you. I loan Cal a ring, a diamond, that I buy at pawnshop. Then I don't see Cal anymore."

Oleg thought of looking behind him to see what was amusing her so.

"Would you loan a dog a steak?"

"Foolish use of good meat."

"Right," she smiled. "By the way, my name's Freddy. Short for Fredericka."

"Is nice name."

"You wanna come in?"

"Thank you, but I must go."

"Where are you from, anyway? Germany or somewhere?"

"No, I am Russian. Oleg Lum."

"Stop hanging on me, Calvin. Go watch TV. Well, if I see Call I'll tell him you're looking. I'd call the police if I was you. No two ways about it."

Oleg took two buses directly to the Adler Planetarium, where something that Carrie had called a "Sky Show" was presented. He sat back in his plush blue seat and looked up as a projector first showed him the sky above the Equator at Christmas and then the North Pole at Easter. He heard names of constellations click in his head like train stops. Oleg watched an eclipse of the moon darken the false sky. He wondered why writers call stars diamonds.

Oleg was sleeping when his doorbell rang. He looked at the Mickey Mouse alarm clock he kept on his bedside stand. It said three a.m. He wandered to the buzzer in his underwear. Keeping his door chained, for who would ring at this hour, he cautiously looked down the hall. Soon he saw Cal walking up the stairwell wearing the same clothes he had on when he disappeared three days ago. He could see the red veins in Cal's eyes and the stubble of beard decorating his prominent, poorly hinged chin.

"Where you were?" he asked Cal.

"I were playing cards, Man," Cal mumbled. In his fatigue, he could hardly get his words out. Oleg had the impression that he was speaking from inside a locked room. "Ain't you gonna invite me in?"

Oleg unchained the door and directed Cal to sit at one end of his hide-a-bed, now open for sleeping. Oleg took the chair opposite. He felt exposed in his underwear and found himself crossing his legs and folding his arms in front of him.

"Practicing yoga?" Cal laughed.

"It is middle of night and I am cold."

"Sure, you was sleeping. Plus, you've given up on me already. You probably called the police."

"I do not call police but I visit Mrs. Weathers on West Jackson Boulevard."

"You visited my mother?"

"I visit a young woman named Freddy."

"Why did you want to see her?"

"I am thinking you live there. I want to see you."

"You're probably looking for this."

Oleg looked in Cal's extended hand. He was holding a ring, but it didn't appear to be Oleg's ring.

"You are magician?"

"What do you mean?"

"You change my lovely Mason ring into this!" Oleg switched on another light and rotated the ring above the bulb. "This ring is maybe glass or even worse." He returned it to Cal's hand.

"Sorry, my man, I got confused with my new wealth." Cal opened another big palm and held up Oleg's original ring.

Oleg placed it on his finger. "Thank you, Cal."

"You can have the other one, too. The gangbanger I got it from says it's real. Take it to your friend at the pawnshop and see. I have to go now."

"See you at work."

"No way. My winnings will last me a month if I'm careful. Perke can shove his oysters you know where." Cal reached around and telegraphed a kiss to his ass.

Oleg spent the next few minutes practicing Cal's obscene gesture. He smiled into the mirror as the ring caught the light of his movements.

THE WINTER BARREL

I remember how everybody seemed to be flowing towards the light coming from a barrel of fire guarded by brown men. The flames peaked for snatches of air. All around were wild children, brown crates and garbage, brown patches of snow and brown mud glistening in the cold. I watched LaNell stand alone as the wild girls passed around her and formed a loose moving gauntlet down the rest of the paved block towards the vacant lot off West Madison with its flame-licked barrel and dazed men.

The tide of battle rose so swiftly, neither the men of the barrel nor the women in the walk-up windows could intervene. But I learned that was the flow of things. I just watched LaNell from the top of the school steps. She looked like a fawn with eyes hard and dark as coals, her lips twisted with annoyance. The first phase of the harassment had mugged the softness from her face. I understood. My innocence, my softness had fallen about the same time as hers—within a week after I arrived from Alabama, the wild children had started in on me—turning my buttery southern brightness all northern blue and porky.

I remembered Alabama and running until my hips hurt and screaming until I was out of breath with joy. Because there, I was warm and everybody knew me. There was a white sun glowing behind the pines. Crickets droning in the quiet. You could walk in the nights fearlessly and the days were full of red clay and green fields for the eyes. Not like this place.

Here you had to kick over a can, toe the trash on the curb, and try to forget the grime and sadness on the edges of everything. What green I learned to see survived between the cracks and along the worn edges of pavement. And it grew up dark, dusty and twisted.

From the top of the school steps looking east in the winter, I felt small, like when I was in kindergarten down south and forced to sit in the back of the assembly hall to watch the school play. The bigger kids in front were always standing up. They were dominating shadows blocking the play, the light from the bright construction paper fantasy on stage. I was too little and too afraid then to make them sit down so I could see. So now all the great buildings before me off West Madison seemed like they would never sit down or sway like those Alabama pines to let the sun through. And at 12 years old I would never see the sunrise over Lake Michigan until I was nearly 18.

So I stood there, looking for something beautiful in the silver wisps gathering in the afternoon sky above the school ground and it reminded me of the long, clear roads in Alabama. We'd be riding in the back of Daddy's pick-up and the pine and spruce looked like they hung from the heavens like curtain fringe. The sun pounded friendly-like on our faces as we juggled around to the road's rhythm. Through the back window of the cab, I'd see Daddy's head and the dark sweat stains ringing the crown of his brown hat, the lighted Lucky Strike poking from his fingers as they gripped the steering wheel, his shimmering blue knuckles, the flying ash.

On third Fridays in the summer, it seemed like all our people in the county gathered at Uncle Ned's and

Aunt Pat's for a party. About sundown, we'd come to this little, weathered, white framed house to eat smokehouse ham and biscuits at the pine picnic table covered with a red vinyl cloth. Uncle Ned always strung up his Christmas lights and everything had an amber, nightclub glow—even the fussy chickens, the dogs lounging around and the hogs that grunted and belched contentedly in the pen back of the house. The song "Finger-poppin' Time" played over and over on the old RCA console in the house. While the card players laughed, loudly slapping down diamonds and hearts, others would dance. The grown folks always looked like they were struggling when they danced, holding each other tight, the sun-bleached clothing on their backs stained with sweat. We kids would dance, too, and dash into the darkness of the adjoining fields to watch the party from a distance.

We watched the men build a great fire in one of Uncle Ned's barrels. They'd drop in great pieces of bark and coax out a flame that nipped and sweetened the velvet air of those summer nights. It was the signal to move in, of welcome, and we kids came running to the gathering around the barrel like little mosquitoes. They never passed us Uncle Ned's moonshine, but there were plenty of gold teeth and pink gums to see. And there was the warmth of big round arms with friendly fingers that fussed with the coarse braids in your hair and called you "baby." All those faces, offended if you didn't look them in the eye and smile. A child could be wide-eyed and innocent. Eyes could be clear and bright. Laughter, open and free.

I knew just where LaNell came from. I saw her when she first moved into the greystone across the street, slowly climbing the steps, staring around and looking surprised by all the winter.

"I betcha this is the first time she seen snow," I whispered to Ma Dear as we peeked secretly through our frosted window. I knew the look on her face. I remembered when Ma Dear and I first got out of Union Station and stepped into knee-deep snow. To me it meant something. When I first felt cold coming up through the sidewalk and saw all these apartments with only windows—no doors—like eyes caged and bolted, I knew it meant trouble. I knew that LaNell wondered what she was getting into—what she was doing here. So when the next day came, which was her first day at school, I asked her.

"Our Papa died," she said. "and so we came to be with our people in the north." She had that happy, talky, friendly way—the way the people are down south. She came from the kind of people who were used to looking you straight in the eye. She was small, but she was alert and wiry, this LaNell. She was dressed real neat, bright and pretty. She wore a nice white scalloped sweater. She smelled well-scrubbed and pure, like baby lotion, and her socks were very clean. She scared me a little when she looked me in the eye. I hadn't seen that for a while. Not since I had made my point the year before and I had to repeat the 6th grade for it. So I was feeling clumsy and inferior next to this girl. She reminded me of what seemed to be a better time, so I liked her. At least she came from a place where people knew some kind of peace. Where people had the decency to leave you alone.

Decency. Ma Dear liked to work that word.

"Decency," she'd hiss. "Decency. These people up here done forgot all about decency."

"Ma Dear, you been up north a long time," I'd say. "What you miss about down south?"

"The colors," was all she'd say and fade into the dark silence of her room that smelled like camphor and rose petals. From then on I learned that sadness was keeping things to myself. I didn't dare tell Ma Dear about my own fights at school.

It was nice to have that moment there with LaNell because she was a person who didn't know the score. She talked to me off and on the rest of the day. I decided to be her secret friend. It was nice—but I stayed alert for the first sign of trouble.

It happened the next day. It was just before noon recess and we were milling around the hallway preparing to go out to the playground. I saw this stupid girl named Tasha all up in LaNell's face. Then she grabbed LaNell's sweater and LaNell pushed her away and started walking in my direction. The bell shrilled. Tasha and her little group of watchers stampeded out of the door for the playground. LaNell looked trapped, her face full of anger and bewilderment. She looked at me with those innocent eyes and said, "Why does that girl want to kick my behind? I don't know her. Why she want to fight?!"

I sensed LaNell was more surprised by Tasha's bizarre behavior than she was actually afraid to fight her.

"Look what she done to my sweater." She showed me a rip along the knitted shoulder seam. That meant even more trouble when she got home. But LaNell, more angered by the trouble Tasha's bullying had caused her, followed the flow of children into the

playground. I saw her charge into a tight swarm of
children circling Tasha. I rushed after her, pushing
shoulders and elbows out of my way. Everybody was
shouting and laughing. I got through in time to see
LaNell nailing Tasha to the asphalt, cold smoke
blowing out of her mouth, tears and snot smearing
her face. One of our teachers wrestled between them
and untangled their bodies. The children shrieked
like birds as LaNell and Tasha were hurried off to
Miss Kruger's office.

At first, I was going to wait for her after school,
but when she didn't come back to class that
afternoon, I knew Miss Kruger had sent her home. I
needed to tell her that it wasn't over yet—that the
worst was yet to come. But when I got home,
LaNell's house was locked up tight. I asked Ma Dear
if she had seen anyone, but she claimed she saw and
heard nothing. I couldn't phone her because she
didn't have one and Ma Dear wouldn't let me go out
to knock on her door. That night, I slept with my
head against my knees, reliving LaNell's predicament
as if it were my own. I wondered if she got a
whipping for her sweater.

In the morning, I saw LaNell in the school
playground with her face pressed against the
hurricane fence. The early sun highlighted her woolly
braids and plastic barrettes. Her face was scorched
with the kind of life-threatening concern uncommon
for a child. She was drawn and ashy, but her strength
was in her anger. Her small knuckles gripped the
fence wires when I told her more was to come. Tasha
was just sent to test her out. Now there was this
other, bigger girl, Rosalind, who wanted to fight her.

"Who are these people? What kinda place is this?"
she asked. "Why can't you just go to school and
mind your own business? Why these people want to
try to jump on you all the time?"

"Yeah, they crazy all right. But that's the way they
use to runnin' everybody around here and just cause
you new and they think you dumb and from down
south, they can run you. But since you got Tasha and
they know you can fight back, ain nobody gonna
mess with you but Rosalind."

"That big, goonie lookin' girl? She look like a full
grown woman."

"She act like one, too. I think something is really
wrong with her mind. I see her hangin' out over
there where those men be at—over by that barrel in
the lot. Ma Dear beat my behind for just standing
over there one time. She say, 'that ain no welcome
barrel, girl. It ain like down south. Decent girls ain
got no business hangin' round over there.' But this
Rosalind, see, I think she killed a baby."

"Naw."

"And she known to carry a knife. She run all the
stupid little people around here. Even boys scared of
her."

"Why she want to stab me?"

"She don't know no other way to be."

"Well, why don't she mess with you then?"

"They did when I first got here. They came after
me in a bunch. I mean they followed me down the
street to my house—callin' me country and callin' my
mama all out her name."

"What did you do? Did you tell Miss Kruger?"

"Who you gon tell? You heard what she said to
you. Shit. That old white woman is scared of these
little wild niggers, too. I made a pact with myself that

nobody was ever gon call my mama out her name.
So I went in the house one day they was chasin' me
and I got me a butcher knife and some hot chicken
grease off the stove and I went out there where they
was standin' in front of my house. And I didn't care
who saw me. I started flinging that hot grease. They
thought I was crazy and they knew I meant
business—nobody wanted to come up against that
grease. Nobody mess with me ever since then."

"I don't like this place."

"They don't neither. But they don't know it."

"I don't like this fightin."

"I didn't neither, but it something you got to
do—unless you want to end up like Tasha and
them—pickin' on folks for ol' Rosalind."

"That big-ass goonie."

"Yeah."

"And she carry a knife."

And with that, LaNell drifted off. She left me
standing by the hurricane fence. I knew how her day
would be—long, torturous and lonely. She was a
small person. The only thing big about her seemed to
be her spirit. I hoped that she would run away and
not be around after school.

As the school day came to a close and the time of
the fight drew near, the memories and meaning of
where I had come from grew stronger. I had to strike
a blow for decency. I remember being mad about not
being able to be a child anymore. I could not show
my innocent eyes or easy smile. Maybe those kids
growing up here didn't understand it, but I knew
LaNell did. It took only 24 hours for them to worry
a hole in her face. I had decided that by the time that
dismissal bell rang I was not going to allow my
conscience or my spirit to freeze like dull snow on a

sidewalk. I decided to take on this second fight to keep these animals from getting the upper hand. If "we" didn't win, at least "we" had to raise doubts in everybody's mind about their power over us. If we didn't, the battle would never end with Rosalind.

So there I was, standing at the top of the school steps looking down at LaNell. She had wasted no time getting outside. I admired that. Underneath, I knew she wanted to cry, but instead of despair, I saw a mask of anger rise and swallow her face. She was going through. She was sending whatever little girl was left in her back to Alabama because she couldn't really live in this place. She had no idea of what she was getting into. I walked down the steps and stood at her side.

"Button your coat up. And put your gloves on," I said. "She really got a knife. Whatever you do—don't let them get your coat off or she'll stick you." I looked down. In the chill, she was wearing some little doll shoes with lace socks and rubbing her knees together.

"I know where she keep her knife. I'll go for the knife. You go for the rest."

LaNell's eyes softened for a moment as if realizing she had been given a great gift. "I want them to say 'You see that LaNell Thomas? Don't fuck wid her. She crazy!'" And we bolted down the street, eluding the patches of ice on the pavement, running, running until our hips hurt—through debris and children yelling wildly toward the vacant lot which was a half-block from the playground. Ahead stood Rosalind, who, at nearly 6 feet tall, towered over the other children. She was gathering her court near the flaming barrel.

Only two or three men were near by, ignoring the onrush of unruly children. I remember how they moved so slowly in relation to our speed. I felt as if we were flying toward the flame they were building with old newspapers, two-by-fours and peanut shells. The misty blue smoke rose against the growing shadows of the afternoon. Their leathered hands trembled as they picked in the ashes with sticks, coaxing the flame, paying little mind to the seriousness of what was about to go down among a bunch of little school girls.

Rosalind seemed caught off guard by our confidence and boldness. I guess she didn't expect me to be in it. She still carried a scar on her hand where I had tossed the chicken grease at her. I immediately went for her coat pocket and snatched out the knife with its worn handle and shiny blade. I heard the smack of LaNell's knuckles land against the bones of Rosalind's face. Rosalind fell to the cold slush and mud. I bounced my shoe off her thigh while LaNell ate up the big girl's head and face with rapid blows.

"Git this bitch off me! Git this bitch off me!" Rosalind screamed to the others who had held themselves back to enjoy the show. But, before they could respond and we'd be grossly outnumbered, I grabbed LaNell's arm and forced her to run with me into the street. Nobody followed. They just stood there looking in awe. The men of the barrel, who had paused to notice our assault for that quick moment, chuckled among themselves as Rosalind struggled to find her feet. The fight was over. The children scattered like last autumn's leaves. The lot belonged to the men of the barrel again and fell silent. Their flames popped and arched, taking a final snip at the cold blue air.

J. Chip Howell

ELMA

—for J.G.

This was her world, alive with city-sounds, the smell of concrete, apartments and closeness. She had once been a part of it, as accustomed to it as she was to her pecan complexion and short hair worn like a tight knit cap. With eyes closed and ears tuned to the jagged chirping of English sparrows, she wondered why was she here.

Elma had always believed that home was a place where you kept a clean wardrobe. But she was home now, drawn to Chicago's back yard by more than just the feel and smell of clean underwear. She wanted to escape what drove her home, but she couldn't, and now, seated before the front window, looking out at the glass-glittered patch of dying lawn she felt the *thing* confront her. It was her most profound fear, the force that drove her before: drove her away from the West Side, with its rundown, shattered buildings; drove her to the South Side, to Judah; drove her to Oak Park, to Asher—quiet Asher; drove her away from Asher, back here, to Austin. She was running out of places and people to run to. She was afraid of being alone.

And she was alone now.

Before any conscious thoughts entered her mind, she was on her feet, trembling over the white phone in her bathroom. It was what she called her "suicide phone," placed just within the enclosure of the room, for easy access when razor blades or pills called seductively to her at the prodding of her aloneness. The number that she dialed lacked the 708 prefix. She was not calling Asher.

After two rings, Judah answered. His voice was more of a sensation than a sound. It touched her ear, then slid into her, fluid-like. Warm.

"Could you come over here, please . . .?" The firmness of her voice startled her.

"Okay," Judah said, with a faint hint of his Spanish accent. "I'm here." He never opened a conversation with a "hello" or "how are you." She stepped aside to let him in. He was tall and lean with keen eyes and hair that reminded her of raven feathers for all the swallowing blackness it possessed. His smile was cunning and his hands terminated in long, tapering fingers that had touched her in ways, gentle in proportion to his strength.

"Thanks for coming. You want something to drink?" She was careful to keep her voice from cracking.

"Diet Coke, if you got it. Water if you don't." He stepped toward the front window and imposed himself against the view of a building on a fast decline. Scrawled signatures and the pale brown remnants of weed growth testified to a reality that Judah was not a part of.

"Is Oak Park suddenly too quiet for you?"

Oh God! He brought it up. Elma cringed and forced herself into the kitchen. She left with two glasses of water, one for Judah, the other for show. She hated water.

Elma shuddered, inhaled deeply and settled onto the couch. Her eyes settled a gaze on the window behind Judah. He stood motionless, back to the view now, hawk-keen eyes fixed on Elma. For a moment it seemed as though he could see straight through her—straight to her reason for calling him here. She cursed silently at his eyes, not so much for themselves, but for what she thought they saw.

"Well?" His question shattered the perversely long silence sprouting from her thoughts, her gaze into his probing eyes.

"Asher and I fought. . . ."

The words came simply: a response without thought, and Judah stood motionless, then looked down into his glass. Her words had some effect on him, it seemed, but she couldn't tell what it was. Damn Judah and his stoicism! She needed an emotional response, some show of human feeling other than Asher's cold, calculated responses to her emotional half of their most recent and heated argument. Why couldn't Judah feel her anger, her loss?

"About what?" Judah's question came gently.

"*Him!*" Elma spat the word. "Me," she said more gently. "He says that he's my best friend, he acts like it sometimes, but most times—when I need him—he's giving his time to someone else; to other friends. Especially Bastien."

"Bastien . . ." Judah sounded as though he was tasting the name.

"You don't know him," Elma said, defensively.

"You don't want me to know him," Judah said, eyes focused on her.

There was no rising inflection, nothing to mark either question or comment in his voice. The ambiguity of his vocal noise made her more angry and confused than she had been during her argument with Asher. Did she want him to know Asher? Did she want Judah to be aware of a man she never thought to introduce him to prior to this?

"I'm sorry," Judah said. "You need to talk."

So she talked, hesitantly at first, then with greater ease. She told of how Asher had drawn her to him some time ago with his oddly youthful looks—his hazel eyes and friendly expression. Her talk drifted toward the bond that she had with him, how she felt that they drew close; near the point of intimacy, but no further. But she didn't say how she wanted him, how she found herself drawn to his whiteness. She hid how she (silently?) demanded that he be equally drawn to her. She felt threatened. Though there were no other women in his life, there was Bastien, that enigmatic friend who seemed to flash into Asher's existence with the suddenness and permanence of some parasitic, psychic presence. Bastien wasn't sudden, Asher explained, he was just suddenly revealed by her unexpected presence. So she reasoned that he was an old psychic leech, dependent on the blood which sustained her.

"You hate him?" This time, Judah's voice was an undeniable question.

"No." That was a lie and she could taste it.

He shook his head, stepped toward her, frowned, then toyed pointedly with the ice in his drink. He was planning something, she knew. He was always calculating, calm, barely emotional. Whenever he played with ice or anything of the sort, he revealed that he was on the verge of making some move with emotional implications he didn't particularly feel comfortable with.

This felt like an argument. She didn't like the warmth this made her feel. It was as if something was breathing down her back—as if Asher's cold words drifted around her now. Dear God, she wanted to escape this, but it came home with her and surfaced with Judah. Her words with Asher drifted though her mind.

—*You ignore me.*—

—*You say that you don't want pay-back for what you do but you constantly remind me of what you've done for me, what I need from you, how good a provider you can be.*—

—*Bullshit, Ash. You do it all the time. You say, "I'm sorry, Elma, I gotta go. Something's up," or "Bastien's on the other line," or even "Bastien's here with me now." Like damn, Ash . . . what's it between you two? Is he giving you head or something?*—

That last question hurt him, strangely, as though it was a truth hurled at him with intent to kill. Had she meant to kill—to hurt him with the force to make his eyes brim with the silvery tears that he'd (accidentally) allowed her to see?

"Elma," Judah said. "Tell me exactly what happened. Talk it all out."

She talked, she spoke her words to Asher again, asked the same questions.

Later, Judah sat, peering directly into her eyes, closer than he had been earlier.

"I'm not judging," he said, "like some daddy figure. But you have to let Asher breathe. He's a friend of yours. You're a friend of his. Let that be, don't demand."

"I'm not demanding. I just want Asher to be with me as much as he's with Bastien. I need him to be there as for me as much as he is for Bastien, too."

Judah shook his head slowly, as though listening to the faint noise of the motion. He was beside her now, on the beige couch, and he seemed more aware of the nuances in his facial movements than he would have been had the two of them been farther apart.

"Suppose I tell you that he is . . .?" Judah's question was cooley stated.

"You don't even know him!" She spat the words venomously.

"But I know you," he responded, almost afraid—it seemed—to release his words. "And that gives you so much of a view into this?" Her words bit, but with less sarcasm than she anticipated. She could see that in the mild discomfort in Judah's dark eyes.

He simply shook his head and drew a shallow breath.

"No," he said, his voice even and unstrained. "I'm not here to show you any insights I might have gained. Nor did I answer your phone call to come here and tell you to just sit back and be glad that Asher pays *any* attention to you. I'm here because you asked me to be here."

That pulled her mind back to the aloneness which prompted her to call him in the first place. Anger surged through her as she thought for an instant that he was gaining control over this situation. Asher had control and was able to maintain it. The last thing she wanted was for him to control this moment now—through Judah. This discussion, though calm, followed the pattern of her past arguments with him.

She focused her thoughts away from that, stepped to her feet and approached the front window. The view beyond was the same as it had been, but there was a timeworn quality, not recognizable until now.

Colors seemed different, textures blurred. The blue/gray cast of the sky appeared faded, and the time-beaten facades of the buildings across the street seemed more solid and imposing.

She felt small. Very small.

And though it hurt her, she thought about Asher, of how she wanted to love him, wanted to share his other-worldliness. This was definitely not his world, and in looking at it now—with its crumbling buildings, shattered glass sparkles and its urban hunger—she began to wonder if this world was hers as well. Sure, she knew Brandon May, who lived in the building across the street and sold snow-cones to children in the summer. And she knew Bethel Raney, who lived two doors down in a building that had many, many ghosts; as many ghosts as shards of glass scattered in the annual greenery that was only partly grass. She knew a lot of things, but could her knowledge of random names and identities insure that she was not as alien to this place as Asher was?

"Elma . . ." Judah was directly behind her now.

"I'm okay," she said.

"Are you sure?" he asked.

The question stung, because she wasn't sure. She wasn't okay. Asher's face flashed into her mind. Their first meeting in a restaurant downtown played and replayed though her memory. If she hadn't spoken to him, hadn't challenged his impetuous gaze that long time ago, would she be feeling lost and frightened now?

"Elma?" He touched her shoulders, her arms.

Silence.

"Elma?" His voice was a whisper now—a sound she needed to hear. She didn't expect to hear it. She didn't want to, consciously, but then she thought back to her call, how it felt to have contact with him, even through the phone.

His hand slid further down, this motion pulled him closer. Now he was whispering lightly, touching her gently, doing precisely what she wanted Asher to do. And it felt like she thought it should.

"Hold me close," Elma said, turning.

Judah put his arms around her, his grasp promising something as fervent and complete as her argument with Asher, but less painful. His expression was blank, as if he intended for his face to express her feelings. She looked into his eyes.

She saw her reflection. Double. Tiny.

He added nothing to what she saw, but then she indulged a thought of desire for him, his blank gaze grew lively. She pressed closer to him, feeling him with herself—not just hands, but breasts, stomach, face, and that place that itched with sudden heat. From what she felt, she knew that Judah had been paying a vast amount of attention to her. He had seen her, all of her. And from his hardness against the source of her heat, she felt that he'd seen enough of the real her to be relaxed enough to want her.

"Judah," she whispered. He made a low noise. She felt it. "Do you trust me?"

He made the same low noise, then kissed her. Yes: he trusted her. He trusted her enough to initiate what she wanted. She kissed back, savoring the moist joining of their mouths, the taste of him. Without another word, she lead him into her room . . . where they met each other with the sounds of breathing. She snagged his button-fly, worked it loose, while he skillfully worked off his shirt, then hers. Cool air touched her bareness, then vanished to the warmth of his flesh. He held her.

She grasped him tightly, then—when naked—moved violently with him. The energy of her angry arguments with Asher bled from inside, spread over Judah, and drove her to muffle his rasping breath with her own passionate sounds. When her anger was nearly spent, she moved more gently.

Afterward, they slept.

She woke to darkness and the sound of her own breath.

She felt the empty bed beside her and was confronted with sudden aloneness. Panic sliced though her, plucked what nerves couldn't be cut and left her cold. Her gaze made connection with various textures in the darkness—the smooth dull orange glow of sodium vapor street lights; the sharp darkness of her own unlit furniture; a sinuous dark form, lean, attractive.

"Judah?"

The figure turned smoothly. "I got restless." Judah sounded apologetic. "I got up to think and see what's going on outside." The faint acoustic signature of his Spanish accent was more pronounced in the dark.

"So, what do you see?"

"You," he answered.

"What kinda answer is that?"

Judah shrugged. "This place is you." He gestured toward the night view. "It's brooding, dark, pent-up. Just look at what's happening out there—it's violent, trapped inside itself, passionate."

"So I'm just like what's outside my window, huh?" she asked. "I'm like the West Side." Elma spoke to the darkness, there was no rising inflection but her words tasted and felt like a question.

"Yeah," Judah said simply.

And that's how she felt about him. From his lovemaking, she felt the release of tension, the shaping of his passion, the hot escape of his anger. From Asher, she felt only cool control, more than Judah ever showed. His chill was deep, and only now did she realize that its depth wasn't intended for her to get through.

"It's chilly in here," Elma said.

Judah stepped toward the bed, settled on it and placed his arms around her. She enjoyed the warmth, but wondered if it could last. Could his warmth, like Asher's reserved coolness, be a source of anguish for her? Was her enjoyment of Judah's warmth just a reaction to her argument with Asher? She didn't want to think of those questions or their possible answers. So she simply let Judah hold her and fulfill her immediate need for a firm, warm touch.

James McManus

MAKING IT TALK

My new girlfriend Linda has just called to tell me she thinks she's been bad. I'm watching the news with the sound off, but the sports is about to come on. There's a catch in her voice I don't like. Burt, my eight-year-old son, is still shooting baskets in my tableless kitchen, providing his own play-by-play. He also makes sure I am watching. Linda works three nights a week as a reference librarian in Skokie, and these are the nights that Burt has been spending with me.

"Just a second," I say, then tell Burt again to go brush his teeth. I've already pasted his brush. "I'm just getting Burt off to bed here."

He dribbles the quarter-scale ball through his legs, "goes baseline under pressure" with an ornery look on his face, "gets triple-teamed and does a three-sixty" as he pushes off under the basket, then spins up a left-handed layup, "making it talk off the glass." It rims around twice and goes in.

"Bad?" I ask Linda.

Burt punches the air with his fist, jerks it straight back, then asks me, "That Mom?"

"Can you talk?" Linda says.

I hold up my fist in response to his layup and shake my head no. It most certainly isn't his mother. "I'll be off in a minute," I tell him. "A figure of speech," I tell Linda. "I just need a second to—"

"Check," she says. "Got it."

Burt rotates the ball in his palms and gives me his look.

"Just go and brush."

He shoots one last turnaround jumper—"Pippen for three at the buzzer"—misses it, "grabs his own rebound, gets fouled."

"Ho, Burt. I mean it. Let's go."

He makes a fast sign of the cross, lines up a free throw, relaxes his shoulders and exhales. Without looking back at me, he swishes the free throw and skulks down the hall toward the bathroom. The ball rolls across the warped beige linoleum, wobbles a little, then stops.

Okay. I put my head back on the arm of the couch, prop up my neck with a cushion, try to sound casually curious. "Motorhead bad?" Like I find it too hard to believe.

"I think so," she says.

I've been calling her Motorhead lately, and thinking of her as Motorhead, because she's planning to buy a new car and has spent the last month compulsively dealership hopping, studying spec sheets and consumer reports, and running on rather incessantly about twin-port injection, powertrain warranties, yen, cams, transmissions, and numbers and angles of cylinders. Motorhead is also the name of a band alleged to be so very nasty and heavily metallic that if they move in next door to you, *your* lawn will die.

"Let me guess. You picked up the five-liter Mustang with the flamethrower decals."

"The what?"

"A Corvette?"

"I haven't decided yet, Ben. I guess I can't deal with the cheeseballs who sell them. So, by the way, how are you?"

I still own half of a lawn and a house, but I just don't go to them any more. Motorhead is also the first girl or woman with whom I haven't been sexually dysfunctional since Leona, my wife, got a boyfriend last spring and formally, through our former lawyer, requested that we be separated. I moved out five months ago Saturday; in a month things will all be official. But I'm already drinking much less, and my extravagantly detailed fantasizing about a reconciliation is more or less over. I've torn up some photographs, too. I've even been getting some sleep, with the help of B complex and Dalmane. I had a few dates before I met Linda, most of them fix-ups by people at work, but none of these ever worked out, including the two with Leona. With Motorhead things have been different. I even have learned how to don prophylactics without losing one reason for wearing them. Sometimes.

"Well," I tell her, "I guess I'm doing fine. How're you?"

"Have you listened to your present yet?"

Two days ago she gave me a battered used copy of *What's Words Worth?*, Motorhead's second live album. It's next to me here on the couch. The cover features a bust of who else with the blade of a shortaxe sunk deep in the top of his skull.

"I'm afraid that I haven't," I say.

"Well, gee," Linda says.

I listen for Burt down the hall. His video hoop game I'd be able to hear from his room, but I don't. Something tells me, however, that he isn't yet brushing his teeth. I pull out the Motorhead liner and read a few lyrics.

Obsequious and arrogant, clandestine and vain
Two thousand years of misery, of torture
  in my name
Hypocrisy made paramount, paranoia the law
My name is called religion, sadistic sacred whore

They are sung by either Filthy Phil Taylor, Lemmy,
or Fast Eddie Clark. The liner notes don't make it
clear.

"Plus I wanted the studio version," I say.

"We'll see what we can do," Linda says, "as long
as you still insist on calling me that."

"So tell me about it," I say. I want to know how
she's been bad.

She asks me instead how my son is. She very much
wants to meet Burt, but I've told her it isn't quite
time yet. The latest agreement I have with Leona is
that we won't introduce him to any third parties till
we mutually agree he is ready. Our principal
criterion—we've actually typed this stuff up—is that
the person will not be a negative influence. Even
Leona admits that she made a mistake by taking him
to the movies with Mel, her third boyfriend, the
week I moved out. We want to expose him to as little
confusion as possible. Plus I figure the longer I hold
out with Linda, the more pressure there'll be on
Leona not to take my son out on her dates or start
having sleepover parties. I hope.

"Burt's not bad," I say, not on purpose. Have
Motorhead's lab tests revealed she has AIDS? Is she
pregnant? I replay the ways this is possible. There
are, after all, one or two. "But so tell me how you
were," I say.

"I just pulled this prank," she announces. "Or
maybe I should say, this stunt." Her accents and

pauses, plus the way she enunciates every last consonant, makes my brain produce aural endorphin, so things she says don't always register. Her voice, as a matter of fact, is the thing that I like most about her so far. It makes her sound fragile but street-smart, high-class, with undertones, hints, of debauchery. She also will holler and bark when we're watching TV and a team plays tough defense. So she doesn't have AIDS, I decide. I sip some more Bushmills and listen.

She tells me a man with a Thai or Vietnamese accent has just called the reference desk and asked her how to spell restaurant. "He was opening one and was painting the sign and writing the menus and he didn't have a dictionary. Either that or he did have a dictionary but he couldn't find the word because he didn't know how to spell it."

"Did he also ask if you had pig's feet?"

"Like I say, I may be dumb, but I'm not pretty."

This is not true. Motorhead looks like a pocket Grace Kelly with bangs. Same cheekbones, same yellow hair, pretty much the same nose and eyes. Not quite as tall, though—not even as tall as Leona—and much plusher torso and lips. "My poor bee-stung lips," she has called them. Her legs aren't long, but she doesn't look bad in black jodhpurs. She is medium vain at the most. She's also terrifically booksmart.

"How about Prince Albert in a can?" I say. I can't help it.

"Didn't ask me that, either."

At least twice a shift, she has told me, she is asked to spell words. She also converts fifths to liters, plots H and D curves, ascertains whether cockroaches have a discernible odor, performs online searches on corporate takeovers, proofreads eleven-page term papers on Hamlet written by fifteen-year-olds, calculates the time in Managua when it's noon in Chicago on May Day, explains how it is that flames won't point down. Once, when a dictionary definition proved inadequate to the task, she demonstrated for a Bahraini sheikh's niece how to curtsy. She also reminds me that polls say librarian is our country's most trusted profession; commodities trader is second to last, behind lawyer.

"Even still. Sort of sounds like the prank was on you."

"It wasn't," she says, rather firmly. "Don't be a dip, Ben. Okay?"

"You say so."

She repeats that the caller was Thai, or Asian at least, and insists that his question was serious. "So listen," she says. "I'm telling you something, okay?"

"Okay." I'm wondering how to spell restaurant, too. So I listen.

"Here's the thing," Linda says. "I looked it up, right? But when I told him how to spell it, I kind of accidentally on purpose transposed the a and the u."

"You didn't."

"I did."

I picture the menu, the sign, the urbane third-world restaurantgoers shaking their heads in bemusement. "Pretty tasty," I say. "Pretty tricky."

"Pretty nasty," she says. Clears her throat. "It's not mine to resist such temptations, I guess. Do you know what I mean?"

Not exactly.

She says, "Just a second, okay?" I hear a male voice ask a question. The next thing I know I'm on hold.

I sip some more Irish and review the warm facts. Four or five years ago my little Motorhead had what is now called a substance-abuse problem. She didn't just say no. She was snorting cocaine for the most part, injecting "the occasional" speedball, and dealing "as kind of a lucrative lark" with her carpenter-skankmeister boyfriend. She has shown me some snapshots. Linda looked skanky but twenty pounds lighter, the boyfriend looked just like Pat Riley, and both of them looked pretty shady. And these are the pictures she's shown me. At some point two sets of unfriendly persons with badges and handcuffs and automatic weapons—serious dealers and officers of the law, it turned out—got involved. But that is now long in the past. No trace of punctures, no love lost—she tells me—on boyfriend, no record. (Her father's a big-time attorney.) Two sets of lab results negative. She got herself clean, went back and finished her master's in Information Science at the University of Chicago, found a good job. About the only substances she abuses these days, to my knowledge, are cognac, champagne, Irish whiskey, an occasional Marlboro Light.

Perhaps it's the interface between time zones and curtsys and speedballs that intrigues me so much. I don't know. I do know I'm terribly fond of the way that her system processes alcohol. A finger of cognac leaves her all flowering wisteria and handjive, and champagne makes her talk like Rosanna Arquette. Even splitting three-fourths of a liter of dark, smoky Irish with me makes her mouth taste like banana yogurt and leaves the rest of her body and brain in a squall of Hibernian candor—instead of all bad blood and bus fumes, like mine. I can only imagine what junk did.

"I'm back," she announces. "Guy wants to know who his congressmen were."

"Who they were?"

"Don't we all?"

"Do we?"

My call-waiting signal cuts in. We ignore it, or try to.

"Forget that," I tell her. "Go on."

"Anyway, Ben, what I'm saying is that, to tell you the truth, I really don't feel so hot about it any more."

Instead of asking when she hasn't been telling the truth, I tell her, "I do that all the time, too."

"You do what?"

"You know. Almost spell it, misspell it, that way."

"Not on purpose, you don't."

This is true. "Though it's not like I have all that many—"

"Just a second," she says, then puts me on hold.

Opportunities. No. There's no action. Maybe half our relationship takes place on the phone at this point, and a third of this time I'm on hold. It's all just a matter of time now. I watch the new president wave from the door of his plane then prick up his ears for a question. I have trouble adjusting my cushion, but I don't spill my drink. I'm not angry any more. It's all just a matter of fact. I wave at the screen, but the president doesn't wave back. Who is he, I wonder. I'm Ben, the pluperfect. I hold.

When I take the receiver away from my ear, I can hear Souled American thump, slide and twang through the wall from Ndele M. Johnson's apartment:

Benny Goodman

He's a good man
What do you think of him?

Ndele's new hillbilly kick doesn't bother me—I
love this stuff, too—except for on school nights this
late when Burt's sleeping over. But right now I think:
boost the bass. Plus it sounds a lot better than hold.
Ndele has fifteen-inch woofers. He has also taught
Burt how to be more aggressive on defense, blow his
nose with one finger, and go to his left off the
dribble.

Motorhead's back on the line. "Can I ask you a
serious question?" Her voice is unhusky, exquisite,
but it suddenly makes me real nervous. Before I can
answer, she whispers, "Have I really been bad, do
you think?"

I'll give you been bad's what I think. I picture the
backs of her knees, the tendons and veins of her arms
and her throat, the small of her marvelous back. Her
"Cowgirl in the Sand" naughty outfit. Her software.
I also can picture her blood backing up behind air
bubbles then spurting out onto her wrist. I think
about thrice-used syringes.

"I'm afraid that you have, Motorhead."

"Do you think I should be punished?"

Do I think she should be punished. Things have
not reached a point where I know what she means by
this word, but I say, "I'm afraid that I do." I also
have trouble remembering how to spell sentence.

"Do you?"

"Don't you?"

"I don't know. Do you really?"

"And how."

"And but, so how?"

I think for a moment. In person, in bed, our conversations do not take these turns. We also don't whisper as much. "How?" I say, sipping and thinking some more. "As in Injun?"

"You mean, like an Indian sunburn?"

"I mean that in due course appropriate measures will have to be taken. This Friday evening, in fact. Maybe running some gauntlet would teach you—"

"Hey Dad?" It is Burt. He has picked up the other extension.

"Hello?" Linda says.

"What's up, Burt?" I say, right away.

"Is there my school tomorrow?"

"Afraid so," I say, sitting up. "Did you brush yet?"

"But so isn't it that, you know, guy's birthday?"

"What guy?"

"You know," he says. Then he says, "Isn't this Motorhead?"

"Motorhead?" I say, though exactly to whom I don't know.

They are silent. They both must be holding their breath. I finish my Irish, suck ice. Is it my imagination or has Ndele just turned up the music three notches? The bass lead is slapping in both of my ears, through the wall on my right and the phone by the wall that is next to Burt's bed, in baffled and out-of-phase stereo.

"Yeah," Burt says, finally. "Motorhead."

"Burt, listen," I say. At dawn I will still be awake. I understand this and accept it. "Hey, Burt?"

They are silent. What's left of the ice zaps my molar. I realize I'll have to go over and talk to Ndele again. Tallulah, a Bloomingdale's model, will answer the door in a T-shirt and kneesocks. Ndele will have on his feedcap and be gnawing a toothpick. They both will profusely apologize, ask about Burt and his schoolwork, turn down the music. Perhaps turn it all the way off. I will apologize, too. Tallulah will mimic Ndele playing air slide-guitar, call him "white bread" or "Leroy" or "big drawers." They will offer me pizza, or bratwurst and beer, some pudding to take back for Burt. They will ask about Motorhead, too, insist that we all see a Bulls game. It will not be unpleasant, I realize. But still.

My call-waiting signal cuts in. I tell Burt, "Hang up for a second, okay?" As soon as he does, I say "Just a second" to Linda and press down the button, relieved to be changing connections.

"It's me," says Leona. Her voice isn't really unfriendly—not deadpan, just dead. Pluperfectly matter-of-fact. "Is Burt still awake?"

I admit it.

"Okay."

When she makes herself talk this strange way on the phone, I always assume she is being undressed as we speak. Does she know this and do it on purpose? I never know what to assume when she talks to me this way in person. I often imagine her pregnant.

All she wants, she is telling me now, is to just say goodnight to her son. Fair enough. She says she's been calling since nine. I decide that I shouldn't dispute this. She does not call me Bosco or ask whether Burt's said his prayers, but it's all just a matter of time now. I pick up *What's Words Worth?* and notice a choice of two fan clubs: Motorheadbangers, whose address is in Leeds, and the Motorhead Appreciation Society, in Dorset. I can't decide which one to join.

"Hold on a second," I tell her, then click back to Linda and Burt. "It's time," I say, "to hang up now, okay?" Has Burt come back on yet? "You know, get some sleep. Your Mom wants to talk to you, too."

They are silent. Cut off, hung up—I don't know. I take the receiver away from my mouth, close my eyes. I wonder who is there on the line, who is coming at me through these dozens of miles of glass fiber, from all these directions, what's words worth. As loud as I can, I call Burt.

"Ben?" Linda says.

"Dad?"

"You okay?" Linda says.

I look up and see my son watching me. Crying? No, coughing. Okay. He looks less like me than his mom in this light. I accept this. Something about where his eyes angle in toward his nose. He stares at my glass on the table, at the Motorhead album at the spiraling powder blue wire that leads to my mouth.

"It is making me talk," I tell Burt. "It's a matter of fact. She's been trying to call us all night. Fiber optics or something. You know?"

He is standing right next to me now, watching the end of the sports. They are flashing the girls' high school volleyball scores. I look at his basketball, there on the floor in my kitchen. Burt is here, too. There is that.

He takes the remote from the arm of the couch and turns on the sound. "I have to call Mom, Dad."

"I know," I say, holding his taut little shoulder. I hear female voices and finger the telephone button. There there.

Burt says, "Okay?" then turns up the sound. One of the anchors has just told a joke. The other one laughs, shakes her head. I shake my head, too, nod at Burt. I am still always here, after all.

"Hello?" says Leona.

"Okay. Just a second," I say.

Burt turns up the sound even further. It's the theme for the end of the news: lots of brass and synthetic percussion. I let go his shoulder and listen.

ELLA IN THE MORNING

You say that you want me—your sister of the heart—to tell your story, but you only want me to whisper it to the wind, the waves, the landscape. So, I commit it to paper, to you, for you, because you cannot bear to hear the words steeped in regret—only bear to see them etched here as though that will take away their bite.

TODAY

Hovering in that valley between sleeping and waking, you reach out for Ella, the one with the see-through eyes and the summer-wheat hair, the one your mother warned you about, the one you were with when you should have been worshipping at your father's shrine. None of your father's relatives—no matter how many times removed from him—will let you forget it.

You reach out for Ella in your North Side apartment that is the size of your old bedroom in your Father's House. You live in Chicago's Lakeview now to prove to everyONE everyWHERE that you are a black woman fully grown.

And when you reach out from the depths of your sweaty sheets, you find your boxes of whatchamacallits and thingamajigs encamped about you like guardian angels, nowhere else for them to go. And the dresser standing at the foot of your sofa bed sticks its drawers out at you like tongues.

"Ella . . ." Your voice trails away like old perfume. She hugs you, trying to understand this fever of remorse.

In your head you can see your father wavering in heated memory, a silhouette in a black and white movie, trench-coated and wearing a fedora. A cigarette perches on his bottom lip. He is Sam Spade. Phillip Marlowe. More than a security guard with a bad back and good intentions.

Behind him stands a woman—your mother yet not your mother. With ghoulishly red lips and stiletto heels, she aims a gun at the back of your father's head and pulls the trigger. Click. Nothing. She aims the gun at you, and words ooze from her mouth. "You should have been there." She pulls the trigger, and you hope that Bang is thunder. It is not, but it is all right to bleed in black and white, you think.

Mama and Daddy are only silhouettes here . . . part of the dreamscape.

But these dreams do not start until the day of the funeral, the day you return to the Neighborhood. Ella cannot come. She wants to come, but your mother forbids it, and you do not wish to argue over the guest list; it would not be proper on the day of the . . . Then you think the truth: You have shriveled in your mother's harsh light.

YESTERDAY

On the day of your father's funeral, your family's apartment is filled with tight-fisted August heat. Open doors and windows and churning table fans won't budge it. It's always too hot when someone you love dies, and the illusion of coolness hangs overhead like the blade of a guillotine. You can see the heat swelling around you. It moves like molasses. Everything is sticky and brown. Nothing is sweet.

"We are all so sorry about your _____." Please fill in the blank: Uncle, Brother, Nephew—ah, yes, Father.

You swallow hard in this place bulging with people you do not know, and try to act your age for your Daddy's sake. He has finally done what he threatened to do for years—simply slip away—and he has taken a piece of you with him.

You anchor yourself to a corner of the kitchen and offer only a nod to those condolence-bearers and finger-pointers. You don't take your hands out of the pockets of your one good suit—a tailored black pin-stripe, an adult gift from Ella—because you do not want to touch them as you remember Daddy. The folks touch you, out of graciousness, out of habit, out of obligation, but those touches slide off your shoulders and down your back and onto the floor, harmless.

While these folks are touching you, you remember slicing open summer with your father, splitting the days right down the center like melons, and those memories linger and mingle uneasily with memories of hospitals and the sharp odor of sickness . . .

You relive the visit of three weeks earlier while the back slaps pile up on the floor around you. Inside your throbbing head you walk into his bedroom again, and the first thing that catches you by the throat is the shadows on the walls, shadows dancing, breathing. Tall white tapering candles—five on each night stand—give the shadows life. No other light is on in the room, and the shades are pulled. Some of the candles stand in cigarette-blackened ash trays;

others rise from freshly washed jam jars. The air is heavy with waxy sweetness, and you want to back out, but you cannot. Propped up on pillows against the headboard of the huge bed, your father has seen you and smiled.

"Come on in, Jordan." He has named his second-born daughter after a river of hope. "Come sit with the old man."

You walk in softly and close the door behind you. Your shadow joins the others on the wall.

"What's with all the candles?" You kiss his forehead. He is half the size he used to be, and he looks twice his forty-five years. His skin feels papery to the touch. You think he will peel away. The bounce of the springs on the bed as you sit is a welcome distraction.

"Your mother has given up on modern medicine and prayer. She has turned to witchcraft."

He laughs. You laugh to avoid his gaze. His eyes have hollowed.

"Daddy, you're kidding."

"No—she brought a healer to the house. Madam Constance. Aargh!" He has one hand across his flannel-gowned belly and another across his forehead. He is Camille. Bette Davis on a bad day. "She's losing her mind, poor woman. Afraid I'm going to die before the mortgage is paid."

"Daddy—you're not going to—die—and you know it." Your words break up like Morse code. "You're—going to—outlive all of—us."

"The doctors don't think so."

"The doctors don't know everything." You take his hand and wonder if it belongs to the same man who walked too fast for you to keep up only a year ago. "Are you—feeling—okay?"

"Am I feeling okay? Well, considering I just got home from the hospital where sadomasochists ripped me open and removed parts of my vital organs, I feel great."

Cartoonish growls follow this, and you let a chuckle spill out onto the crisp white sheets. He is so dark against the covers.

"Can I get you something, Daddy?"

"No, no. I'm doing okay, sugar. I've got my wife, my children—and sixteen candles on my cake." He sings this last part raspingly and waits for your smile. "How are you?"

"I'm okay." You shrug.

"Just okay?"

"Well, I'm better than okay."

"You'd better be. You're still in school, right?"

"Yes."

"You're still going to be a teacher, right?"

"Yes."

"There's no money in that, you know?"

You smile because he always says that.

"I know."

"I'm proud of you, but you could be a doctor like your sister."

He is baiting you. He knows you cannot tolerate hospitals because—well—because they are full of sick people. Dying people. Your sister serving time in medical school is made of steel, but you are only sand. She does not ask why the members of your family go into hospitals and never come out whole.

"One doctor is enough."

"Maybe you'd do better as a mortician. If Melba can't cure them, you can bury them."

He reels you in.

"I'll stick to English Lit, Daddy."

"Fine, but there's no money in that. If J.T. had finished college, he would have been a lawyer. There's money in law."

"Yes." You do not want to think of J.T. now. You want to face one loss at a time.

"How's Ella?"

Surprise—a snag in the line! None of the family ever talks about that well-mannered white girl who laughs too loudly and dresses down unintentionally. Your mother ignores her. Your sisters ignore you. Your brother smiles at her as though all this pretty grad student needs is a REAL MAN to reshape her life. Now your father recognizes Ella as real and not a group hallucination.

"Ella's fine."

"I only met her a couple of times, but she seems real nice. Ella's special to you, isn't she?"

You bite your lip. You look around the room and try to find the right words in the wallpaper with rain-soaked ducks; in the open closet with the authentic military uniform from one of the truly big, truly important wars; in the antique furniture creaking and dusty-looking in spite of your mother's constant cleaning; in the pictures gleaned from the suburban garage sales and flea markets, tinted photographs of serious-looking people you will never know. No words are found. The truth must do instead.

"I love her."

"Your Mama doesn't approve."

"I know."

You shrug, and you watch him shrug.

"I just want you to know that I love you, Jordan."

This is all he says. He offers none of his love to
Ella, none of his support to her, but he gives it to you
to share with her, and you promise to come back to
see him. You do not make it.

You visit Ella's well-meaning parents in
Washington, D.C., for a week instead, and no one
will let you forget. How dare he die!

Now in their Sunday-go-to-meeting clothes, people
pause in front of you. They say something to you,
but you cannot hear them above the lip-smacking,
soda-guzzling consolation of the other guests. They
stand elbow to elbow, chicken wing to chicken wing,
all waiting to touch you, their caresses filling up the
room.

Women wearing white gloves and veiled hats and
men holding hats in their hands seem to sprout from
the walls, the furniture. They are almost funny as
they appear like Clay People in old episodes of
"Flash Gordon." Soon they will spread like kudzu
vines onto the porches and into the streets.

Suddenly your mother grips your shoulder. You
cannot let it slide into the pile with the other
unwelcome touches.

"What are you doing in here, Jordan?"

Her mouth is twisted between grief and anger, and
she contains herself only long enough for the guests
to lick their fingers and return to the living room.

"You've been blind. Are you deaf now, too? I'm
talking to you, Jordan."

"I heard you."

"And?"

"And what?"

"And why are you here when you should be out
there?"

"I shouldn't be anywhere except where I want to be." The softness of your voice surprises and calms you. "I only came here for Daddy—not for you or Melba or Buddy or Sylvia. For Daddy. So, I guess I should go."

"You guess you should, do you?" She tightens her grip on your shoulder. "It's funny to me how you've learned how to run out on us. Who taught you that? Ella?"

"Ella? I almost said something stupid like, 'Please leave Ella out of this,' or 'She has nothing to do with this,' but she has everything to do with this, doesn't she?"

You jerk away your shoulder, but the pinch of those fingers lingers.

"Yes, she does. You changed when you met her, that little white girl."

"Oh, that's it. I'd be okay if I just fell in love with black women."

You think she is going to strike you, but she does not. You flinch, but her raised hand brushes through her graying hair.

"You're so different now. As much as we love you, you've abandoned us for some—woman."

"I haven't abandoned you."

She continues as though you are no longer there, as though her truth will make you swallow every one of your LIES. You reach for her shoulder this time, to steady her, but she turns toward the sink, and you can only listen to her tiny sobs, gasps really, as she explains to somebody beyond the kitchen window how things are now.

"When Joseph Tyrell died, you weren't there either. Your own brother, and you were having dinner with Ella."

"J.T. died playing basketball. None of us could've known—"

"His heart just exploded. Then your own daddy."

"I loved him, and he loved me—"

"No, you'd rather scrape together plane fare to visit Ella's family. You saw her family more than you saw this one. You love her more than you love your own family, your blood. And I wonder what I've done to deserve this. Haven't I suffered enough? I couldn't depend on J.T. Then your daddy dies on me. And now I'm supposed to just welcome this woman—this poor little rich white girl—"

"She's not rich."

"—into my house. Why don't I just blow my own brains out?"

"I love you, Mama."

". . . my own brains . . ."

This is the last you say to her. That is the last you think you will say to any of them as you slip out of the kitchen, through the spreading vine of satiated mourners, out of the apartment, and into the street. Buddy waves from the porch as you scatter the children lying over the hood of your car. It is too dark to tell if he is smiling, but he must be. It is what he does best.

TODAY

You are away from the buzz of pity surrounding your father and you must rise from your own depths. You wonder who is kissing you into consciousness. Ella. It is morning, and Ella is standing on the surface of your waking, and you know that you do not love her for her see-through eyes and summer-wheat hair.

"Ella . . ."

She squeezes you, strokes you, loves you. And waits for you to break through the fever of regret. You are not sorry for yourself or even for your Daddy whose suffering is mercifully over.

You are sorry for those left behind as the catalysts of their own despair.

Mark Allen Boone

BRUNSWICK STEW

"Fooled them suckers," he said, returning to the living room and removing a half pint of whiskey from his coat pocket. "Spread some bread at the foot of a tree and waited for 'em to come down."

Lutie's pity was torn between the two bloody squirrels that lay on the sink's apron and her new husband, Elmo, who had no conception of Chicago's ordinances. It would do no good to explain to a man who'd lived sixty-eight years by instinct that killing city squirrels might be against the law. She wouldn't try. Nor would she eat them, for in doing so, she'd be giving her tacit approval. Their half-closed eyes were eerily accusing. No, she'd simply watch Elmo dress, cook and eat them himself, suffering quietly as the aroma wafted throughout the three-room flat.

She had made some creditable gains in her year-and-a-half-long marriage to Elmo, the janitor at True Vine Missionary Baptist Church. She'd taught him how to write his name, how to dial the local emergency telephone numbers and how, after countless trips on the Ogden Avenue bus, to find his way downtown. But lately she worried about him, especially since the tumor in her abdomen had been diagnosed as malignant. Lately her thoughts were centered more on how he'd manage in an increasingly complicated world than her exit from it.

Six months earlier, when Lutie had first learned about the malignancy, she refused to accept the fact that she had cancer. She had noticed the slight swelling in her stomach but shrugged it off as only

85

fluid retention. After all, hadn't she been on water pills for years? In the early stages of the illness, she felt no real discomfort at all.

Elmo, studying her stomach every day suggestively asked her if she hadn't some "news" to tell him. Lutie was too outdone by the thought to be humored by the idea that she might have been pregnant. She was sixty-six years old! But Elmo said that according to the Bible, older women than she had given birth. Well, she certainly wasn't going into another record book, Lutie vowed. And after she had gone to another doctor for a second opinion and had the test results confirmed, Lutie couldn't decide for sure whether Elmo's disappointment was because of the cancer or because he wasn't as potent as he'd thought he was.

When her doctor had trouble communicating to Elmo the seriousness of her illness, Lutie volunteered to break the news to him herself. It was natural for her. She'd explained so many things to him since they'd been married.

"You not goin' no place," Elmo declared when Lutie told him. "They don't know what they talkin' 'bout. You need some healthy food, that's all. Been eatin' poor food too long. People in Mississippi never caught a lot of cancer. It's 'cause they raised they own food. They knew what they was eatin'," he asserted.

"I know about raising food, Elmo," Lutie said. "I lived on a farm down South, too," she reminded him.

"Well, you forgot how to cook it," Elmo said. "Been up North too long to remember. I'm cookin'

you some squirrel stew," he said one day after Lutie
had come home from her chemotherapy treatment.
"It'll bring your strength back."

"I haven't had Brunswick stew since I was a girl,"
Lutie said. "I didn't think people cooked it
anymore."

"I don't know nothing 'bout no Brunswick stew,"
Elmo had said. "All I know 'bout is squirrel stew.
Baby, it's so good, it'll make you eat yo' head off!"

"Elmo, the name for any stew with squirrel meat
in it is 'Brunswick' stew. Honey, that's all I'm
saying."

"Well, I'm being straight with you," he replied.
"So it won't be no surprise. I don't b'lieve in
springin' surprises—trickin' people into eatin'
somethin' they don't want to eat. Did I tell you 'bout
the time I got tricked?"

Lutie had heard the story at least once a month.
Elmo's frequent retelling of the incident was a sign to
her that senility had come in, sat down and crossed
its legs for a long stay.

Forty years before in Mississippi, a neighbor,
without telling Elmo what it was, had asked him to
sample a piece of meat to see if she had put enough
seasoning on it. He was hungry, so he didn't ask
what he was tasting, he'd said. For all he knew, it
might've been rabbit or squirrel. But after he had
swallowed it and licked his fingers, the woman
informed him that he'd eaten a taste of wood rat,
which people were known to eat in certain parts of
Mississippi. He took pains to explain to Lutie that
wood rats weren't real rats—that they belonged to a
different family, but still, he wouldn't eat them.

Lutie recalled her struggle to keep a straight face
as Elmo demonstrated how he stuck his fingers down

his throat to bring the meat up but couldn't upchuck for the life of him. The laughing cook had told him that the meat was too good for the stomach to turn loose. Then Elmo showed Lutie how he drew back and, with his fist, knocked the woman onto the porch floor, breaking her jaw so that she had to have it wired. It was the first time he'd ever hit a woman, he declared, and the last time he'd eaten anything without being told what it was. But Lutie said that just because the cook told you a dish was one thing, it didn't mean that it couldn't be something else. It was all a matter of having faith, she said.

That morning, after he had brought the squirrels home, Elmo opened the back door onto the porch, where he spread newspaper so he could dress them. Normally, he field-dressed his game, he explained, but this time he couldn't take a chance on getting caught on park district property with the two dead squirrels.

Lutie lay on the couch in eyeshot of the back porch, watching him with work gloves on cutting the squirrels to the tailbone. The gloves, he had told her, protected him from catching rabbit fever. Now how he could get rabbit fever from dead squirrels, Lutie didn't know, but she didn't question him about it. She turned her head and winced as he cut one squirrel's pelt the width of its back. Pressing her hands against her stomach, she suppressed a retching impulse.

From her position on the sofa, Lutie studied every movement of the bantam, bashful man who had to muster the nerve to tell her to her face that she was a "fine figure of a woman." Although she was three years Elmo's junior, a maternal protectiveness came over her as she watched him move around in the kitchen—the same maternal feeling that her sister Frannie claimed made Lutie abandon all reason in marrying a "slow wit."

The two of them had a falling out over those words. To that day, Frannie didn't even know Lutie had cancer. Lutie didn't have to explain her actions to anybody, she maintained. Having lived alone for fifteen years since her first husband Eldred died, she had longed for companionship. Just because Elmo didn't read the daily *Tribune*, except to circle the lottery numbers that he played faithfully, or just because he couldn't talk about the issues of the day like Eldred could, it didn't mean that the two of them had nothing in common. At least Elmo loved her. Never before in her life had a man picked wildflowers for Lutie. Never had Eldred told her that she was a "fine figure of a woman" when Lutie knew she had long ago been jacketed by unwanted weight. Elmo treated her in the manner of a man who had panned for gold all his life and who had finally hit a mine when he had given up hope. So she worried about him constantly, fretted about whether or not he'd find a new mate as patient with him as she tried to be—a woman who would be as appreciative of him as he was of her.

Lutie watched him at the threshold of the back door as he stepped on a squirrel's tail and pulled the skin from its body as easy as peeling a sock off a foot. Elmo always killed gray squirrels, he explained, because the red ones had too gamy a taste. At the kitchen sink she saw him cutting up a hen that would go into the stew. He had set out three cupfuls of lima beans overnight so they could soak. Sister Perkins from the church had brought him a paper bag full of vine-ripened tomatoes from her garden. He had skinned them and cut them into small pieces. Another old bag who sang in the Doctor Watts choir at True Vine, and who never even spoke to Lutie, sent Elmo a bushel of corn for "ailing Sister Waters." He had husked enough ears for three cupfuls and piled them onto a piece of wax paper.

Lutie knew that these women didn't have her interests at heart. They were just trying to get in good with Elmo, trying to build up credits so they could stake first claim on him when she was gone. Well, it wouldn't work. Elmo wasn't studying any of them. He had told Lutie so himself. And Lutie believed him.

What a good cook Elmo was! she thought. A much better cook than she was. He never had to measure anything. Instinct told him in what proportions to combine the ingredients. It wasn't Christian-like, she thought, for her to refuse to eat, to spurn the meal he was so carefully preparing. But Lutie had to admit to herself that it wasn't the sad-eyed squirrels so much that made her balk at eating Elmo's stew. It was her resentment of Elmo messing around in her domain, taking over her kitchen when she was too weak to put one foot in front of the other. Elmo was doing for her when she had been so used to doing for him. She knew she should have praised high heaven for him, but all Lutie could see was that this man, about whom knowledgeable people declared she had brought a long way, was functioning in her kitchen as if she were already gone. He didn't need her. That was the final blow, the last indignity. The only way she knew to banish the thoughts that had crept into her heart was to place the blame for them squarely where they belonged: on the Devil. It was Satan who made her feel this selfishness and ungratefulness. It was a good thing that Reverend Goodloe would be over later to help her fight him.

Elmo came out of the kitchen to join her, fluffing her pillow as she tilted her head forward. He pulled an old patchwork quilt over Lutie as she stared blankly at the wall. The quiet rumbling of the lidded pot on the kitchen stove sounded strangely like the bubbling in her stomach that made her feel so bloated. She watched as Elmo sat in the chair across from her and rolled the butt of a dead cigar along his gums. Respectful of her feelings, he had been smoking it outdoors since he knew that the smell nauseated her.

"Rev'n Goodloe'll be over this evenin'," he reminded her. He took the cigar out of his mouth, lay it on the jar-lid ashtray and picked up the *Tribune* that she had half-read earlier.

Good old Rev'n Goodloe, Lutie thought. If it hadn't been for him, Elmo wouldn't have the job at True Vine. She was thankful for him. He was a good pastor. A faithful steward, just like she considered herself to be.

"Think Rev' Goodloe'll have supper with us?" Elmo asked.

"There's plenty of it to go around," Lutie said, careful not to betray the fact that she had no intentions of eating any. She watched him write something on a piece of paper. He stared at the writing as though, like a hieroglyphic, it had some hidden message. He then folded it back up and stuffed the scrap of paper in his shirt pocket.

"What number you playing, Elmo?" Lutie asked.

"Seven seventeen," he answered. "Same number that's go'n win me the money to buy us a house an' a piece of land where we can raise our own food."

It was the same number that he played when Lutie had first met him. She didn't know whether there was anything magically connected with it in Elmo's mind or not. Once, when the winning number was seven twenty-seven, Elmo whooped and hollered as if he'd won. When she reminded him that he hadn't, he said that at least he'd come close. Lutie couldn't convince him that in a game of chance there was no such thing as coming close. Either you had the number or you didn't.

"Elmo," Lutie said, as he folded the paper. "We've gotta talk about how you're gonna get along when I'm gone. We gotta talk about who's go'n see after you."

"You ain't going nowhere," Elmo said.

He was catching a cold and as he snorted up the running phlegm, the whistling sound made his head ring hollow.

"Elmo, don't bury your head in the sand. Look at you. You can't even take care of a cold. Snorting like a horse. I can't do everything for you. I'm not always gonna be around."

"Yes you will," Elmo said. "I'm fixin' you some squirrel stew. It's go'n knock that sickness right outta you."

He went over to the couch and grasped Lutie's hand. His short fingers were the color and thickness of the cigars he gummed. Such big hands for such a small man, she thought. And yet he'd never raised once against her. Was as gentle as a baby. She'd never have believed that he had broken a woman's jaw if she hadn't heard it come from his mouth. Maybe

Reverend Goodloe could talk to him for her. There wasn't anything else she could say to Elmo. She'd given him all she could give and had nothing more stored away.

Reaching over the coffee table for her medicine, she took two capsules from a white bottle and pressed them onto her tongue. Elmo held her up as she swallowed the water he brought her.

"I'm tired, Elmo," she said. "So tired . . ."

"Go on and rest," he said, easing her head onto the pillow. "When you wake up I'll have your stew ready for you on the table. It'll be just right for you to eat."

Lutie slept fitfully, drifting in and out of consciousness so often that she wasn't sure if the indistinct vision of Reverend Goodloe seated in the chair across from her was real or imagined.

"Why'nt you tell me Rev'n Goodloe was here?" she asked Elmo when she awoke. "I'm not even decent," she complained, rearranging the covers around her and adjusting the wig on her head.

"I didn't want to 'sturb you," Elmo said. "You was restin' so peaceful."

"I wasn't resting peacefully," Lutie snapped. "I was drifting in and out."

Reverend Goodloe came over to the couch where she lay. He was a tall, double-jointed man with pitying eyes and prayerful hands. When the congregation at True Vine got caught up into one of his frenzied sermons, the faithful sisters swooning in spasms of joy, he'd strut across the pulpit, flapping the long black sleeves of his robe like they were wings.

"I come to have fellowship with you, Sister Waters," he said.

"Elmo, get my Bible," Lutie said. "I want to follow 'long with Rev'n Goodloe."

Elmo went into the bedroom and soon brought out a heavy, ivory-colored Bible with gold leaf along the edges of the pages. After he had given it to her, he went back into the kitchen to check on the stew.

"Rev'n Goodloe," Lutie addressed him in a low voice, "I'm worried about Elmo. He's come a long way in the time we've been married. What's gonna become of him now?"

"No need of you worrying about Brother Waters," Reverend Goodloe said, moving closer to the couch. He sat on a hassock that Elmo had pushed beside it. "The Lord looks after His own."

"Reverend Goodloe, he went out and killed squirrels today. Park squirrels. He's making a stew. You don't go around killing city squirrels," she said.

"People killed pigeons during the Depression," Reverend Goodloe said. "They were good eating, too."

"They did it because they had to," Lutie answered. It was a matter of survival. Elmo don't have to. We've got plenty of meat in the freezer."

"He told me he was fixin' you some squirrel stew to bring your strength back," Reverend Goodloe said. "He told me how he killed those squirrels and how he scraped together the makings for the stew. His faith is so strong that it puts mine to shame."

"But Rev'n Goodloe, that's just my point," Lutie explained. "Brunswick stew and nothing else is gonna make me better, but I can't get him to see it. He's got the mind of a child."

"You knew it when you married him, Sister Waters," Reverend Goodloe said. "Let him believe what he wants to. It's the least you can do for him."

"But I can't sit back and let him go off on the wrong track," Lutie replied. "I've brought him a long way. I'm responsible for him. I taught him how to sign his name. I showed him how to ride the bus downtown . . ."

Elmo appeared at the doorway. Lutie sent him away with a wave of her hand, signalling that she and Reverend Goodloe were having a private conversation. Reverend Goodloe began reading one of Lutie's favorite passages—The Beatitudes.

"Blessed are the merciful, for they shall be shown mercy. Blessed are the pure in heart, for they shall see God . . ."

He was soon interrupted by a clinking noise from the kitchen. It was Elmo using a spoon as a clapper inside an empty jar announcing that the Brunswick stew was ready to eat.

Lutie sat propped up in the kitchen chair like a doll invited to a fake meal. For her, the dinner might just as well have been for play because her plate was the only untouched one at the table. She stared at it as if her eyes could make it disappear. Reverend Goodloe, exuberant at stumbling upon a free meal, ate heartily, greedily spooning the stew into his mouth.

"Haven't had Brunswick stew since I was a boy," he said. "Elmo, you really put your foot in it, didn't you?"

Elmo dropped his head bashfully and continued to eat, mincing the meat finely with a fork.

"You waitin' for yours to cool, Baby?" he asked Lutie. "It's cool enough for you to eat now."

"I don't have an appetite, Elmo," she said. "I'm nauseous from the chemo treatment."

"You missing a real treat," Reverend Goodloe said. "It's so good, your tongue'll slap your brains out!"

"You two help yourselves," Lutie said. She put her hand to her chest to suppress a rising wave of nausea.

"Anybody who can cook a meal as good as this don't have to be worried about," Reverend Goodloe said. "Elmo, you missed your calling. You shoulda opened you a restaurant."

"It still ain't good enough to suit Lutie," he said.

He covered his face with his hands as though he couldn't stand to look at Lutie and her untouched plate of stew. Lutie heard the familiar adenoidal snort that sounded so much like a burst of air into an empty bottle. Elmo wouldn't show the tears that she knew were there. He kept his hands in front of his face and inhaled with a whistling sound.

"I wouldn't poison you, Lutie," he said. "You know that."

"I believe that any treatment that keeps a person from enjoying food ain't much of a treatment," Reverend Goodloe said. "Eating's one of the natural pleasures of living."

Elmo didn't talk. He had finished his plate but didn't go back for another helping. Reverend Goodloe eyed Lutie's plate covetously as though he were waiting to be told he could have it.

"I know how Elmo feels, Sister Waters," he said. "His feelings are hurt. What if you spent the whole day cooking a meal that somebody you care for refused to eat?"

Elmo took Reverend Goodloe's plate and went into the kitchen to refill it.

"It's not the stew," Lutie said in a low voice. "And I have been nauseous. But I can't lie to you, Reverend Goodloe. The truth is I can't get used to Elmo doing for me. It hurts me not to be able to get up and do the things I used to."

It was hard for her to explain that she wasn't used to having Elmo worry about her. Difficult to explain to Reverend Goodloe that she resented her husband, envied him even. She had always done the worrying in the house. She had been his eyes, ears and mouth for the past year-and-a-half. It had given her a reason for living. Her overwhelming sense of duty outweighed the need for her to love Elmo. He had been her cause. His progress had been the fruit of her good works—the works that would be her passport to heaven.

"Let Elmo take care of you," Reverend Goodloe said. "It's his turn, now. You've got to give him his chance."

Elmo returned to the table with Reverend Goodloe's plate and a piece of cornbread.

Reverend Goodloe touched Lutie's hand and guided it to the unused spoon that lay beside her plate. She lifted the spoon and submerged it into the stew, bringing up vegetables and broth to her lips. Opening her mouth, she emptied the spoon and swallowed hard, like a child taking unwanted medicine. Dipping her spoon, she fished around for a piece of squirrel meat. When she found a morsel, she lifted it up, put it into her mouth, chewed and swallowed it, feeling the lump travel down her throat.

"You don't have to eat that cold stew, Baby," Elmo said. "I'll bring you some hot from the stove."

He left and returned to the table with a large pot. He ladled a steaming plateful in front of Lutie and refilled Reverend Goodloe's plate.

"Help yo'self," Elmo exclaimed. "It'll give you strength."

The spoonfuls of stew did give Lutie strength, though maybe not the kind that Elmo had in mind for her. Little by little, the nourishment gave her strength to believe. To believe that everything would work itself out. To believe that she could fall back weakly and let Elmo take care of her in her time of need.

She swallowed a spoonful of stew, then another, and another, all the time reflecting about the ingredients that went into it. Lutie would ask Reverend Goodloe to pray for her and Elmo before he left. She'd ask especially that he pray that Elmo would store up the love she felt for him and, in the habit of the squirrels whose flesh they feasted on, would unearth it in the cold lonely months ahead.

"Rev'n Goodloe," Lutie said after she was halfway through her refilled plate, "Keep those corn-giving buzzards away from Elmo when I'm gone. I know they're just waiting to close in after the kill. Keep 'em away from him cause I know he won't have strength enough to fight 'em all off by himself."

Elmo grinned. "Lutie Mae, I keep telling you, you ain't going nowhere," he said.

Tony Ardizzone

NONNA

She has seen it all change.

Follow her now as she slowly walks down Loomis toward Taylor, her heavy black purse dangling at her side. Though it is the middle of summer she wears her black overcoat. The air conditioning is too cold inside the stores, she thinks. But the woman is not sure she is outside today to do her shopping. It is afternoon, and on summer afternoons she walks to escape the stifling heat of her tiny apartment, the thick drapes drawn shut to shade her two rooms from the sun, the air flat and silent, except for the ticking of her clock. Walking is good for her blood, she believes. Like eating the cloves of *aglio*.

She hesitates, the taste of *aglio* on her tongue. Perhaps she is outside this afternoon to shop. She cannot decide. The children of the old neighborhood call out to her as she passes them. *Na-na!* The sound is used to call in goats from feeding. Or, sometimes, to tease. Or is it *Nonna*, grandmother, that they call? It makes no difference, the woman thinks. The thin-ribbed city dogs sniff the hem of her long black dress, wagging their dark tails against her legs. Birds fly above her head.

Around her is the bustle of the street corner, the steady rumble along jounce of cars and delivery trucks, the sharply honking horns, the long screeching hiss of a braking CTA bus. The young men from the Taylor Street Social and Athletic Club seem to ignore her as she passes. They lean against streetlight poles and parking meters in the afternoon

99

sun. One chews a cigar; another, a toothpick. One walks in front of her, then turns to the gutter and spits. The woman looks into their faces but she does not recognize any of them, though she knows they are the sons of the sons of the neighborhood men she and her Vincenzo once knew. Grandsons of *compari*. Do they speak the old language? she wonders. Like a young girl, she is too shy to ask them.

One boy wears a *cornicelli* and a thin cross around his neck. The gold sparkles in the light. Nonna squints. Well, at least they are still Catholics, she thinks, and her lips move as she says to herself, They are still Catholics, and her hand begins to form the sign of the Cross. Then she remembers she is out on the street, so she stops herself. Some things are better done privately. The boy's muscled arms are dark, tanned, folded gracefully over his sleeveless T-shirt. The boy has a strong chin. Nonna smiles and wets her lips in anticipation of greeting him, but his eyes stare past her, vacantly, at the rutted potholes and assorted litter lying next to the curb in the street.

She looks at what he stares at. He grunts to himself and joins his friends. On the shaded side of Loomis is the new store, a bookstore. The letters above the front window read T SWANKS. Could the T stand for Tonio? she wonders. She crosses the street. Then it should properly be an A. For Antonio. Anthony. Named for any one of the holy Antonios, maybe even the gentle Francescano from Padova. Nonna always preferred the Francescano but never told anyone. He had helped her to find many lost things. She believes that if she were to speak her preference aloud she would give offense to all the others, and what does she know of them—Heaven is full of marvelous saints. Her lips whisper Padova.

The sound is light. Nonna enjoys it and smiles. She pictures Padova on the worn, tired boot. Vincenzo called Italy that. Nonna remembers that Padova sits far up in the north, west of Venezia. She looks down at her black shoes. Italia. She was from the south, from Napoli, and Vincenzo, her husband, may he rest, came from the town of Altofonte, near Palermo, in Sicilia. The good strong second son of *contadini*.

A placard in the bookstore window reads FREE TEA OR COFFEE—BROWSERS WELCOME. Nonna is tempted to enter. She draws together the flaps of her black overcoat. She could look at a map of Italia if the store had one, and then maybe she could ask Mr. Swanks for which of the Antonios was he named. And what part of the boot his family came from, and does he still speak the old language. She does not realize that T Swanks might not be the name of the store's proprietor. She assumes that, like many, Swanks is an Italian who has shortened his name.

Beneath the sign in the window is a chess set. Its pieces are made of ivory. The woman stares at the tiny white horse. It resembles bone. She remembers the evening she and Vincenzo were out walking in the fields and came across a skeleton. That was in New Jersey, where they had met, before they came to Chicago. She thought the skeleton was a young child's—she flailed her arms and screamed—but then Vincenzo held her hands and assured her it was only an animal. Eh, a dog or a lamb, he had said, his thin face smiling. Digging with his shoe, Vincenzo then uncovered the carcass. It indeed had looked like a dog or a lamb. That was a night she would never forget, the woman thinks. And that smell. *Dio!* It had made her young husband turn away and vomit.

But Nonna is certain now that what she saw in that field that dusky autumn evening had been a child, a newborn *bambino*, clothed only by a damp blanket of leaves. The Devil had made it look like a dog! New Jersey was never the same after that. She made Vincenzo quit his good job at the foundry. They had to go away from that terrible place. Nonna openly makes the sign of the Cross.

She knows what she has seen. And she knows what kind of woman did it. Not a Catholic, she thinks, for that would have been the very worst of sins. It had been someone without religious training. Maybe a Mexican. But there hadn't been any Mexicans in New Jersey. Nonna is puzzled again. And all Mexicans are Catholics, she thinks. Each Sunday now the church is full of them. They sit to the one side, the Virgin's side, in the back pews. Afterward they all go to their Mexican grocery store. And what do they buy? Nonna had wondered about that all during Mass one bright morning, and then from church she had followed them. The Mexicans came out of their strange store talking their quick Mexican and carrying bananas and bags of little flat breads. Great bunches of long bananas. So green—

Maybe Mexicans don't know how to bake with yeast. Nonna realizes her lips are moving again, so she covers her mouth with her hand. If that is true, she thinks, then maybe she should go inside Mr. Antonio Swanks's new bookstore and see if he has a book on how to use yeast. Then she could bring it to the Mexicans. It might make them happy. When they kneel in the rear pews, the Mexicans never look happy. Nonna shifts her weight from foot to foot, staring at the little white horse.

But the book would have to be in Mexican. And it would cost money, she thinks. She does not have much money. Barely enough for necessities, for neckbones and the beans of coffee and *formaggio* and *aglio* and salt. And of course for bread. What was she thinking about? she asks herself. Did she have to go to the store to buy something? Or is she just outside for her walk?

She looks inside the bookstore window and sees a long-haired girl behind the counter. Her head is bent. She is reading. Nonna smiles. It is what a young girl should do when she is in a bookstore. She should study books. When she is in church, she should pray for a good husband, someone young, with a job, who will not hit her. Then when she is older, married, she should pray to the Madonna for some children. To have one. To have enough. Nonna nods and begins counting on her fingers. For a moment she stops, wondering where she placed her rosary.

No, she says aloud. She is counting children, not saying the rosary.

Nonna is pleased she has remembered. It is a pleasant thought. Five children for the girl—one for each finger—and one special child for her to hold tightly in her palm. That would be enough. They would keep the girl busy until she became an old woman, and then, if she has been a good mother, she could live with one of her sons. The girl behind the counter turns a page of her book. Nonna wonders what happened to her own children. Where were Nonna's sons?

She hears a shout from the street. She turns. A carload of boys has driven up, and now, from the long red automobile, the boys are spilling out. Are they her sons? Nonna stares at them. The boys

gather around the car's hood. One thumps his hand
on the shining metal on his way to the others. One
boy is laughing. She sees his white teeth. He
embraces the other boy, then throws a mock punch.
They are not her sons.
   She turns back. It is clear to her now that the girl
has no children. So that is why she is praying there
behind the counter! Nonna wants to go inside so she
can tell the unfortunate Mrs. Swanks not to give up
her hopes yet, that she is still young and healthy, that
there is still time, that regardless of how it appears
the holy saints are always listening, always testing,
always waiting for you to throw up your hands and
say *basta* and give up so that they can say, heh, we
would have given you a house full of *bambini* if only
you had said one more novena. Recited one more
rosary. Lit one more candle. But you gave up hope.
The saints and the Madonna were like that. Time to
them does not mean very much. And even God
knows that each woman deserves her own baby.
Didn't He even give the Virgin a son?
   Poor Mrs. Swanks, Nonna thinks. Her Antonio
must not be good for her. It is often the fault of the
man. The doctors in New Jersey had told her that.
Not once, but many times. That was so long ago. But
do you think I listened? Nonna says to herself. For
one moment? For all those years? My ears were deaf!
Nonna is gesturing angrily with her hands. She
strikes the store's glass window. It was part of
Heaven's test, she is saying, to see if I would stop
believing. She pulls her arms to her breasts as she
notices the black horses. They stare at her with
hollow eyes. Inside the bookstore the manager closes

his book and comes toward the window. Nonna
watches her close her book and stand, then raise her
head. She wears a mustache. It is a boy.

Nonna shuts her eyes and turns. She was thinking
of something—but now she has forgotten again. She
breathes through her open mouth. It was the boys,
she thinks. They did something to upset her. She
walks slowly now to slow her racing heart. Did they
throw snowballs at me? No, it is not winter again.
Nonna looks around at the street and the sidewalks.
No, there is no snow. But she feels cold.

Then they must have said something again, she
thinks. What was it? Something cruel. She stops on
the street. Something about—

The word returns. Bread.

So she is outside to go to the bakery. Nonna
smiles. It is a very good idea, she thinks, because she
has no bread. She begins walking again, wondering
why she had trekked all the way to Taylor Street if
she was out only for bread. The Speranza Bakery is
on Flournoy Street, she says aloud. Still, it is pleasant
today and walking is good for her heart. She thinks
of what she might buy. A small roll to soak in her
evening coffee?

The afternoon is bright, and Nonna walks up the
shaded side of Loomis, looking ahead like an excited
child at the statue of Christopher Columbus in the
park. She likes the statue. Furry white clouds float
behind the statue's head. Jets of water splash at its
feet. She remembers the day the workers uncovered
it. There had been a big parade and many important
speeches. Was there a parade now? Nonna faces the
street. There is only a garbage truck.

So it must not be Columbus Day. Unless the
garbage truck is leading the parade. But it is the

mayor who leads the parade, Nonna says, and he is not a garbage truck. She laughs at her joke. She is enjoying herself, and she looks again at the green leaves on the trees and at the pure clean clouds in the blue sky.

The mayor, she hears herself saying, is Irish. Nonna wonders why Irish is green. Italia too is green, but is also red and white. The garbage truck clattering by her now is blue. So many colors.

She thinks of something but cannot place it. It is something about Italians and the Irish. The mayor. His name. He cannot be *paesano* because he is not from Italy. But she knows it is something to do with that. At the curb alongside her a pigeon pecks a crushed can.

It is Judas. Nonna remembers everything now. How the mayor unveiled the statue and then switched on the water in the fountain, how all of the neighborhood people cheered him when he waved to them from the street. All the police. Then the people were very angry, and the police held them back. Where did they want to go? Nonna thinks, then remembers. To the university, she says, to the new school of Illinois that the Irish Judas had decided to build in their neighborhood. The mayor's Judas shovel broke the dirt. And then, one by one, the old Italian stores closed, and the *compari* and *amici* boxed their belongings and moved, and the Judas trucks and bulldozers drove in and knocked down their stores and houses. The people watched from the broken sidewalk. Nonna remembers the woman who had tapped on her door, asking if she would sign the petition paper. The paper asked the mayor to leave the university where it was, out on a pier on the lake. Was that any place for a school? Nonna asked the woman. The woman then spoke to her in the old language, but in the Sicilian dialect, saying that Navy Pier was a perfectly good place. Then why build the school here? Nonna said. Daley, the woman said. Because of Mayor Daley. Because he betrayed us. Because he wants to destroy all that the Italians have built. First on the North Side, with the Cabrini Green projects, he drove us out. Now he wants to do it again here. He wants to drive us entirely from his city, even though we have always voted for him and supported his political machine. Sign the paper. If you understand me and agree, please sign the paper. For a moment Nonna thinks she is the woman. She looks down to see the paper in her hands.

There is no paper. The paper had not been any good. The men in the street had told Nonna that. Shouting up to her windows, waving at her with their angry fists. She had yelled from her windows for them not to make so much noise. Two men tried to explain. Then what is good? Nonna had asked them. You tell me. I want to know. What is good? She is shouting. A car on Loomis slows, then passes her by and speeds up.

These, the men had answered. Rocks. Nonna is afraid again as she remembers. She had pulled her drapes tightly shut. But still from behind her open windows she had been able to hear all through the long night the shouts of the men who kept her awake and the rocks, rocks, rocks, thrown at the squad cars patrolling the streets and through the windows of the alderman's office.

She hears the water. Splashing up to the feet of Christopher Columbus, the boy who stood at the sea's edge thinking the world was round like a shiny new apple. Nonna knows history. She memorized it to pass the citizen test. Columbus asked himself why he first saw the tall sails of approaching ships, and then the apple fell from the tree and hit him on the head and he discovered it. Nonna is smiling. She is proud that Columbus is *paesano*. Sometimes when she studied and could not remember an answer, she would hit herself on the head. That knocks the answer out of sleeping, she says. Though sometimes it does not, and Nonna thinks of her own head, how once it had been full of answers, but now many answers are no longer there. She must have lost them when she wasn't looking. Should she pray to Saint Antonio? But he helps only with things, with objects. Maybe, Nonna thinks, when she puts something new inside her head, something old must then fall out. And then it is lost forever. That makes sense, she says. She laughs to herself. It is the way it is with everything. The new pushes out the old. And then—she puts her hands to her head.

There is only so much here, she says. Only so many places to put the answers. Nonna thinks of the inside of her head. She pictures brain and bone and blood. Like in the round white cartons in the butcher's shop, she says. The same. She makes a face. All those answers in all those little cartons. Suddenly Nonna is hungry. She wants a red apple.

A group of girls sits at the fountain's edge. Nonna hears their talk. She looks at them, cocking her head. Did they just ask her for an apple? Someone had been asking her a question. I don't have any, she says to the girls. She pats the pockets of her black coat. See? she says. No apples. She wonders what kind of girls they are, to be laughing like that on the street.

They must be common, Nonna thinks. Their laughter bounces up and down the sunny street. Like

Lucia, the girl who lives downstairs, who sometimes sits out on the steps on summer nights playing her radio. Nonna often watches the girl from her windows; how can she help it, the music is always so loud. A polite girl, Nonna thinks, but always with that radio. And once, one night when Nonna was kneeling in her front room before her statue of the Madonna, she heard Lucia with somebody below on the stairs. She stopped praying and listened. She could not understand any of the words, but she recognized the tone, and, oh, she knew what the girl and the boy were doing. The night was hot, and that brought back to her the thin face of her Vincenzo, and she was suddenly young again and back in terrible New Jersey, in her parents' house, with young Vincenzo in the stuffed chair opposite her and around them the soft sound of her mother's tranquil snoring. Nonna shakes her head. She knows what she must feel about that night. She was trusting, and Vincenzo was so handsome—his black curls lay so delicately across his forehead, and his smile was so wet and so white, bright—and she allowed the young boy to sit next to her on the sofa, and she did not protest when he took her hand, and then, when he kissed her, she even opened her mouth and let his wet tongue touch hers. Oh, she was so frightened. Her mouth had been so dry. On the street now she is trembling. She is too terrified to remember the rest. But the memory spills across her mind with the sound of the girls' easy laughter, and she moves back on the pink sofa and does not put up her hands as Vincenzo strokes her cheek and then touches her, gently, on the front of her green dress. And then she turns to the boy and quickly kisses him. The light from the oil lamp flickers. The snoring stops. She looks at Vincenzo, and then she blushes with the shame of her mortal sin, and now if Vincenzo does not say they will marry she knows she will have to kill herself, and that in God's eyes she has already died.

Nonna is still, silent, standing in her guilt on the street, afraid even now to cross herself for fear she will be struck down. She feels the stifling weight of her sin. Vincenzo then moved back to the stuffed chair, coughing. Neither spoke. She began to cry. The next morning, Vincenzo spoke to her father.

There are boys at the fountain now, talking. Nonna looks up from the crack in the sidewalk she was staring at. The girls sit like bananas, all in a bunch. One of the boys flexes his arm muscles, like a real *malandrino*. The girls look at him and laugh. Nonna recognizes Lucia. She wears a tight pink top and short pants. Why doesn't she hear Lucia's radio? Nonna wonders. A voice inside her head answers her questions. Because the girl is with the boys. And when you are with them, Nonna says out loud, you do not need the radio.

They look up. Nonna knows she must avoid them. They heard me, she whispers to herself, and now they will throw apples at me. Santa Maria, *madre di Dio*. She feels awkward as her feet strike the pavement. From behind she hears them calling.

Nonna! Hey Nonna! Who were you talking to? Hey, Nonna!

Nonna begins to run, and as she does her heavy purse bangs her side, up and down, again and again. Then the sound of their laughter fades away, and Nonna slows, feeling the banging inside her chest. Now they heard, she thinks, now they know my sin, and they will tell everyone. And then everyone, even the old priests here in Chicago, will know. I'll have to move to another neighborhood, she tells a fire hydrant. I'll pack my pans and the Madonnina and flee. But I have done that already two times. First, from New Jersey, and then when I was punished by the machines who flattened my house down. Nonna does not count the move from Naples, when her family fled poverty and the coming war, nor the move from her parents' house when she married Vincenzo.

He would not have wanted her to be so lonely, she thinks. She is lucid, then confused. Vincenzo understood why she could bear no children; it was because of their sin. Perhaps now that everybody knows, she thinks, she would not have to move any more. Maybe since the whole world knows, I can finally rest where I am now and be finished with my punishment. And then I'll die, Nonna says. And then, if I have been punished enough, I will be once again with my Vincenzo.

Her legs turn the corner for her. They are familiar with the streets. Nonna is on Flournoy, across from the church of Our Lady of Pompeii. At first the building looks strange to her, as if she were dreaming. The heavy wooden doors hang before her inside a golden cloud. She walks into the cloud. It is the blood in her head, the bone and the brain, she thinks. She pictures the fat butcher. The church's stone steps are hollowed, like spoons. Again she feels hungry. As she walks into the sunlight she wonders why she is wearing such a heavy coat. Nonna asks the door her questions. The doors stand high before her, silent. She pulls on their metal handles. The doors are locked.

She could go to the rectory and ask the priest for
the keys. But they never give them to me, Nonna tells
the doors. The priests tell me to come back for the
Mass that evening, and I ask them if they don't think
the saints and the Madonna are lonely with no one
praying to them in the afternoon, and they say there
are people all over the world who are praying, every
moment of the day, but I don't believe it. If it was
true, it would be a different world, don't you think?
She presses her cheek against the wood. Don't you
think? she says. Don't you understand me?

Then she hears something behind her and she
turns. A dog. Panting before the first of the stone
steps. Its ears are cocked. It is listening. Nonna
laughs. The dog gives her a bark, and then from the
middle of the park across the street comes the sound
of a boy calling. He jumps in the sun, waving a dark
stick. Nonna points to him. The boy is dark, like the
stick. A Mexican. So it is a Mexican dog. And
Nonna says, I would tell you that boy wants you, but
I don't know Mexican, and if I spoke to you in my
tongue from Napoli you would just be confused. The
dog turns and runs, as if understanding. Again
Nonna laughs. What is she doing at the top of the
stairs? She knows the church is kept locked in the
afternoon because of the vandals. Haven't the priests
often told her that?

Her hand grasps the iron railing. She must be
careful because of her legs. They get too tired from
all the time holding her up. When she reaches the
sidewalk she stops and faces the church and kneels,
making the sign of the Cross. Then she walks again
down Flournoy Street.

Why was I at the church? she thinks. She makes
the sign of the Cross and then smiles as she walks

past the rectory, and now she remembers the church-basement meeting she attended because of the paper she signed. It is good to sit with *paesani*, she thinks, and she pictures the faces of the neighborhood people, then the resolute eyes and mouth of the woman who gave the big speech. How much intelligence the woman has! Nonna notices that her hands are moving together, clapping. It is good to clap, good for the blood. She stops. But only in the meetings. The woman had said once and for all that it was the mayor's fault.

Vincenzo, Nonna whispers. She sees his still face sleeping on a soft pillow. His mouth is turned down into a frown. Vincenzo, I tell you, it was not your fault.

Nonna closes her eyes. She feels dizzy. It was the meeting, all the talk, the smoke. Then she realizes that was years ago, but she feels she had just been talking with her Vincenzo. Had he been at the meeting? No. Vincenzo died before the neighborhood changed. Before the students came. The *stranieri*. Before the Mexicans crept into the holes left by the *compari*. Then she must be walking home from Vincenzo's funeral. It was held at Our Lady of Pompeii. No, she had been driven to the cemetery in a long black car. Where is home? she thinks. Where am I walking to? And she pictures the faces of her parents, the rooms in the house in Napoli, the house in New Jersey, Vincenzo's house, the house in Chicago and the dust and the machines. Then—

Two rooms.

Nonna remembers where she lives.

So. She must go there. She worries that she has left something burning on the stove. Was it neckbones? Was that what she had taken out for her supper? Or

was it meat in the white cartons? Had she bought
brains? She cannot think. Her legs are very tired. She
will eat, if it is time, when she gets home.

The color of the sky is changing, and the traffic
grows more heavy in the streets. It must be time,
Nonna says to herself. She wishes to hurry so she
won't be late. She does not like to eat when it is dark
out. When it is dark she prays, then goes to bed.
That is why there is the night, so people have a time
for that.

Nonna approaches the street corner, and when she
sees a woman coming out of a doorway with a bag
full of groceries she remembers that she is out
shopping. So that is why she has worn her heavy
coat! But first she took a walk. The afternoon had
been very nice, very pleasant. Did I enjoy myself? she
thinks. It is difficult to decide. Finally she says, Yes,
but only if I can remember what I am outside
shopping for. What is it? It was on the tip of her
tongue. What was it that she needed?

She turns at the door, and as she opens it she
realizes that this is no longer the Speranza Bakery. It
is now the Mexican food store. She is frightened. Her
legs carry her into the store. The dark man behind
the counter looks up at her and nods. Now she
cannot turn around and leave, she thinks. She hopes
the Mexican will not ask her what she wants. What
would she say? Her feet move slowly down the first
aisle. Her hands draw together the flaps of her coat.

Well, she thinks, I must need something. She does
not want a can of vegetables, nor any of the juices in
heavy bottles. She sees the butcher's case and tries to
remember if she needs meat. Then she pictures
neckbones in a pan atop her stove. She must hurry,
she thinks, before they burn.

Cereal, vinegar, *biscotti* in paper boxes. Cottage cheese or eggs? Nonna's heart beats loudly when she sees the red apples, but she remembers how difficult apples are to chew, and she is too impatient now to cut them first into tiny pieces. Nonna smiles. Vincenzo had always said she was a patient woman. But not any longer. Not with hard red apples and a sharp knife.

Then she sees the bananas and, excited, she remembers.

What she needs is next to the counter. In plastic bags. Nonna is so happy that tears come to her eyes. So this is why she was outside, she thinks, why she is now inside this strange store. She had wanted to try the freckled Mexican flat breads. Hadn't someone before been telling her about them? Nonna holds the package in her hands and thinks. She cannot remember, but she is sure it had been someone. The woman with the petition paper, or maybe the girl who prayed for babies in the bookstore. Someone who explained that her punishment was nearly over, that soon she would be with her Vincenzo. That there were the breads that were too simple to have been baked with yeast, that these did not rise, round and golden, like other breads, like women fortunate enough to feel their bellies swell, their breasts grown heavy with the promise of milk, but instead these stayed in one shape, simple, flat.

The dark man behind the counter nods and smiles.

Perhaps, Nonna thinks as her fingers unclasp her purse and search for the coins her eyes no longer clearly see, perhaps bread is just as good this way.

S.L. Wisenberg

AT THE ROSE OF SHARON SPIRITUAL CHURCH, CHICAGO'S WEST SIDE:

hearing Steve Cokely, just fired as mayoral aide because he gave sermons in Louis Farrakhan's church, accusing Jewish doctors of injecting black children with AIDS, among other charges

It is dusk. I have never been to the West Side before. I have been through it, past it once or twice, and one time pointed out a few sights from a window on an architectural tour. This is a bad neighborhood—a poor black neighborhood—empty storefronts, bad schools. Danger. I live north and east, in a mixed but mostly white area: well-kept apartments, cafés, occasional gang graffiti, bad schools. I was driven here by Ann, a journalist, who's a friend of my friend Bill's, a photographer who follows controversy. Andy, another journalist, sits in front. This is history, news. We are recorders of the news—curious, white. The other three have followed the story for days—press conferences in City Hall, denials, accusations, finally the firing. Ann's an editor, Bill takes pictures, Andy covers the Midwest for an Eastern newspaper. I write stories, poems and articles. I freelance. I take rides when they're offered. Andy and I are Jewish. We met on Yom Kippur, the Day of Atonement, in South Florida five years ago.

There are other journalists here. They are white. The people to be observed are black. They are angry.

Outside the church, before the speeches begin, a man tells me he is a Hebrew, a universalist, not Jewish. Like Joseph in the Bible, he is black. Blacks are the true Hebrews described in the Bible—despised, downtrodden. He points to his dark skin, to the skin of the dark men around him. This is the meaning, he says, of Joseph's coat of many colors. Jonah was black too, he says.

I don't care. I don't believe in Joseph and Jonah as historical figures; they are metaphors. I say, The god of the Bible is too hard for me to accept. Patriarchal. I declare my disbelief to this stranger, who asks if I consider myself to be Greek. Greek? He tells me about the Greek translation of the Bible, concludes something from this that I can't follow. Am I Greek or not? He pushes me to declare. What are my origins? Pressed, I say Eastern European. I don't tell about my absurd nostalgia for the Moldavian city, Kishinev, that my family left two generations ago. But I am not Eastern European. I am American, North American, a norteamericana who has learned how dangerous words can be. I have learned that Zionism has become a dirty word. Two decades ago, in childhood, it was naive, plain, boring, as in "Zionist youth group." Eretz zion. The land of Zion. But even then, holding the memory of an ugly threat: "The Protocols of the Learned Elders of Zion." A hoax of a book, popularized by Henry Ford, among others. Some Jews won't buy Fords, still. Mistrust burned into us.

When I go inside to sit down the man next to me says, "I can't sit here," and he moves up a row. He can't sit next to me. What have I done to him? But what has the black man done to me, the black stranger that makes me flinch as I walk at dusk in

Rogers Park? We have made each other into monsters. Or symbols. My skin means power. And I know whites who flinch under the hands of black doctors, who won't vote for blacks (avoiding all names that sound like early presidents: Washington, Jefferson, Madison). I know whites—Jews, one particular Jew, an elderly cousin, actually—who trusts no outsiders. This is nature's law, according to my cousin: The gentile will say he's your friend, but you can't count on him.

I know white Christians who say worse.

I know all kinds who work their whole lives as bridges. Not many.

A man three rows behind me cries out: "Jew busters! Jew busters!" What does that mean? I want to turn to him, to offer myself as challenge or maybe sacrifice. To say, "What will you do to me?" Here I am, the vilified, horned Jew. As I have been for centuries. I want to offer myself, to shame him, them, because he would do nothing, now. It is not dangerous here. There is a crowd, media, witnesses.

At the altar a man in a purple print shirt recites the Shema, a classic Jewish prayer declaring the oneness of God. His style is rough reggae staccato. The second section of the prayer is the Vyahaftah, the prayer that some Bat Mitzvah partners fight over; the one with the best voice gets to perform it. He's saying it wrong, his foreign stresses rendering it all but unrecognizable. This man calls himself a black Hebrew. I know the Shema of the Diaspora, North American-accented. He could be saying it the way the Sephardic Oriental Jews say it, for all I know. His accent could be Israeli.

He is angry. The people here are angry. *Jew busters, Jew busters.* At the altar now the Reverend

Al Sampson is disparaging our six million. He says
that we disparage their 125 million who died as
slaves. Later I hear that a better estimate is
somewhere between 30 and 100 million. A man in
the audience disputes that six million Jews died in
Hitler's camps.

How do you compare destruction?

Steve Cokely is speaking now. He says: "We never
did anything to you."

From the audience: "Yet, yet."

What have I done?

So easy to be the innocent, so easy to say: During
your 400 years of slavery, we were living across the
ocean—studying, trading, fleeing our own
persecutors. It is not our fault. Are my hands
bloody?

And they could answer: But your whole life you
have benefitted from your white privilege.

And then? And then? Should I dedicate my life to
seeking economic justice and freedom, to reaching
across barriers? I do that, a little. Could do more.
But what to do about these people here who are not
my enemies? Who send forth conspiracy theories
constructed of wind and loose threads? Conspiracy
theorists who point fingers at me, at my people?

The man outside told me he doesn't know his
great-great-grandfather. He said, "You probably
know yours, or you could ask your parents." Almost
as an accusation. Almost as if to show me: *See how
deracinated we are.*

My mother knows of her grandfather—he was a
blacksmith. I have relatives with charts that lead
back to Ireland and Spain. On my father's mother's
side, I could get names and dates. My father knows
whom he was named for—his grandfather—knows

the date of his death. That's all. Dead end on my father's father's side, beyond two previous generations. We do know that they were lucky. They lived through the brutal Kishinev pogrom of 1903.

The attacks came from the altar: names of Jews, hurled, as if being Jewish is an indictment. Proof of power, inordinate and preemptive. Prove someone is Jewish and that's all you have to do. Because that in itself is bad. Because Jew equals Israel equals South Africa. Therefore we are all racist, we are in control—watch out. I have read of Israeli cooperation with South Africa, rumors of nuclear sharing. I have read an essay that named three pariah states: Israel, South Africa and Taiwan. Strange ménage. I acknowledge Israel's maltreatment of Palestinians, but would not call it apartheid. American Jews do not equal Israel. American Jews are American Jews. Varied though not numerous.

Meanwhile, the cameras are recording. A newscaster winds up his report on tonight's speechifying and outrage, pronouncing: "But it doesn't stop the problem."

What is the problem? Steve Cokely?

The problem is the unfairness of history. Says a highly excitable man, as lights shine and film turns: "You mistreated us for 400 years and you want us to apologize."

Both are true. They were mistreated and we want them to apologize. If you were mistreated for 400 years, then can you say whatever you want? Because we were mistreated for thousands of years, can New York Mayor Ed Koch say what he wants? Because there are more Jews in New York City than in Israel, can Koch say it is only a crazy Jew who would vote for Jesse Jackson?

The problem is the unfairness of the present. The problem is too big to say simply.

The people in this room are afraid and angry. The activist Marion Stamps says, "If we don't stand up with Steve tonight, they're going to attack us." Sampson says, "If they come for Steve tonight, it will be you and you tomorrow night, Lu Palmer by midnight . . . Farrakhan early in the morning."

The rhetoric reminds me of the famous quote by the minister Martin Niemoller, who said that when the Nazis came for the communists he didn't speak up because he wasn't a communist. And when they came for the trade unionists and the Jews and the Catholics, he didn't speak up. And by the time they came for him, there was nobody left to speak up.

But the people taken away in Germany were not just fired from city jobs. They were killed.

Cokely says, "They want us to look fanatical, kooky." He says, "I was too powerful in government. And don't think they didn't know it."

But he was not fired because he was powerful. He was fired for what he spread. This is what the papers say: This man said that Jews were conspiring internationally. He said Jews were inoculating black children with the AIDS virus. He said public schools were dangerous. At the Rose of Sharon, he tells us that whites took words he spoke to the people of his "house" and took the information to their "house"—to hurt him.

There is so much hate swirling about the room. *Jew busters! Jew busters!* They challenge Jews to a debate. About what? About our innocence? We are innocent. We shouldn't have to prove it. They feel innocent, too. We both feel wounded.

In the car, my friend Bill asks, "Did you feel threatened?" No. Is this how Jews felt in Germany 55 years ago? Unable to imagine that anyone could harm them? I feel foolish, alarmist. This is America, not Germany. And yet, they are preaching the same hatred. But to call them "Nazis" would be fanning the flames—of the fire they started—I am not part of a conspiracy.

After his brothers sold him, Joseph became a famous man in Egypt, advisor to the king. When there was a famine in Israel, his family came to join him. Joseph's people became numerous and strong. They had their own customs. The pharaoh decided they had to be watched, controlled, enslaved. I know this story by heart. This is the story of my people, if I choose to believe it. According to the man outside the church, the people in question were blacks, not Jews. If this were proven scientifically, would it make a difference to me? I don't think so.

Did you feel threatened?

"No. Because of the media," I say. Cameras make things safe. Relatively, not always. And white men. Feminists would point out that I am under the protection of white men. It is true. I am weak. Though I have trained in nonviolent civil disobedience, I am a karate class dropout.

Did I feel threatened? No, not personally. And I feel safe enough now, in the car, going east to the Loop. We are out of earshot. The small intense crowed left behind. The ghetto out of the way. Did I feel threatened? No. But though I have seen no blood, no riot, no mob, no burning, no swastika, the lights of the city tonight seem especially fragile, especially small.

A few weeks later I'm in City Hall and I see a man standing at the foot of the stairs talking to a small group. He is familiar—bow tie, striped shirt, suit. Cokely. If there were other members of the press around, I would take out my notebook and melt into the crowd of listeners. But these are obviously cohorts. They are laughing together. Upstairs, no one in the press room cares. Old news. An hour later, as I'm leaving, he's still there. I want to say, "Hello. I've written about you. Hello. I'm Jewish. Hello. What do you want of me?"

Is it a challenge I want to deliver? To show him up morally? Do I want to hold out my hands so that he will see that they are not the hands of an imperialist?

But I say nothing, and go on to the rest of my errands downtown—go to the office, the cash machine—not declaring my innocence, not delivering a challenge, not extending a hand, not making a greeting of any kind.

THE ONES YOU LOVE,
THE ONES YOU NEED

There's a click from the kitchen, then that tiny squeal. Now I'll have to go clean it up again, quickly, before my baby brother gets in there. Not that he's really a baby, but four is a curious age for a boy and Freddy's likely to think a mouse in a trap can be fun.

"Fuck," says Ruben, our older brother. He's messing around in his room; I can hear him pulling open his dresser drawers one at a time. Ruben's seventeen—two years older than me. He's smart but not that smart, with a bony body and big Bambi eyes that all the girls like.

"What's the matter?" I ask as I pass his door, which is shut and probably bolted.

"Nothing," he yells. But I hear something heavy fall to the floor and then his swearing again.

The kitchen is dark but I don't need a light. I know exactly where I laid the traps. We catch enough mice that I can tell when I hear the snap whether it's behind the garbage, in the cabinet, or between the stove and the refrigerator. This time it's under the sink, where the pipes make a tiny hole through which the mice come.

"Hey baby, what's going on? It's pitch black in here," says Angel, one of Ruben's friends. He flicks the light on, a fluorescent tube with a twitch. Angel's got a toothpick in his mouth and a few stray hairs on his face which he calls a moustache.

125

"Turn the light off," I tell him. I put on my mouse gloves, then reach for the trap. Its prey is still wiggling on the plank.

"Man, that's disgusting," says Angel, averting his eyes. He finally turns the light off.

"This ain't Lake Shore Drive," I tell him. "You don't have mice at your house?"

He shrugs and picks his teeth some more. He's just standing in the doorway waiting for Ruben, who's still shuttered in his room making nervous noises. Ruben's supposed to share his room with Freddy, but he comes and goes, making a racket at all hours, so Freddy winds up sleeping with Mami and me in our room. This way, Ruben gets his own room by default.

"Watcha gonna do with that?" Angel asks, nodding at the mouse as I walk by him.

"Flush it down the toilet, what else?" I say. "Freddy will get to it in the garbage."

"Jesus, doesn't that clog the pipes?" he asks.

I shrug. Angel follows me to the bathroom, where I undo the trap and the mouse falls with a squeak into the toilet bowl. It's just a baby mouse, smaller than my little finger, and when I flush, its eyes bulge before it disappears in the whirl.

"You shouldn't do that," Angel says, following me back into the kitchen where I reset the trap and put it back under the sink.

"Got any other suggestions?" I ask him a little sarcastically. I pull off the gloves and wash my hands, scrubbing them with dish-washing detergent. "We tried fumigating but it didn't work. The guy who came out said we'd have to do it twice a month 'cause all of Humboldt Park is 'rat invested'—that's what he called it. But we don't have rats, just mice."

Angel chuckles. "I don't think you should kill 'em at all." He winks at me.

"Since when are you such a humanitarian?"

He laughs. "Fuck, I'm no humanitarian. I think mice are disgusting. But, hey, if you got so many, you may as well go into business, you know?"

Now I laugh. "What, a mice factory?"

"Hey, why not? You know what? Anglos, man, they have mice as pets. I used to go out with this white chick from the North Side, and her little brother—I'm not kidding you, man, I'm not kidding—he had mice. Kept them right in his room in a cage and everything."

"Get out of here, Angel," Ruben says, shoving him as he comes into the kitchen. He's got a big bulge under his shirt, right at his waist. I hope it's not what I think, but I'm too scared to ask.

"Hey, man, I swear, this Anglo chick's brother had mice, like they were a delicacy or something."

"Delicacies are something you eat, Angel," I say, trying to relax while drying my hands.

"Hey, you know what I mean," he protests.

"Angel, man, what's this bullshit about you dating a white girl, huh?" Ruben says, grinning. "Which lifetime was this?"

"Wait a minute, Ruben, you calling me a liar?"

"Not a liar, man, a bullshitter!" Ruben and I look at each other, laughing.

"Hey, man, you know the truth. You know it was just last year, man. I went out with that girl from Lakeview High."

Ruben turns to me. "You gonna be home tonight?"

"I've got a bunch of homework," I say, looking in the direction of the kitchen table where my books are neatly stacked. I'm finished for the night, but I'm not confessing.

"Great," Ruben says. "So when's Mami home tonight? She working, or out with that dude—what's his name?"

"Eduardo the Dominican."

"Yeah, him," Ruben sniffs. Like me, he hates Eduardo, a swarthy little hospital orderly who keeps following Mami home. She works in housekeeping at St. Elizabeth's, just a few blocks away. Lately, she's been letting Eduardo the Dominican in for coffee and talk. Two nights ago, she went to a restaurant with him.

"She's working," I say. "She should be home in an hour or so."

"That soon, huh?" Angel asks, shooting my brother a worried look.

"What's going on?"

"Aw, nothing," Ruben says, squeezing my shoulder. "The usual bullshit. You going out tonight for any reason?"

"Maybe to the store later, I don't know."

Ruben looks around, as if we're standing at a busy intersection, and he pulls me aside, almost whispering. "If you go out—now you listen to me, Estela—you wear black, understand?" He holds my chin and looks right at me. "You go out just like a nun, okay?"

"Okay. But why?"

"Why?" Ruben sighs. We don't talk like friends do, but we communicate all right. He doesn't hide much; I just have to ask.

"You gotta promise not to tell Mami, okay, because I don't want her to worry," he says, still looking around. Angel paces behind us, keeping guard in the hallway.

"I mean, I heard that there might be some shit going down tonight. So just don't go out, okay?"

"Yeah, but you know Mami's gonna want me to go to the store and buy her cigarettes when she gets home."

"Tell her she should stop smoking," says Angel. His entire body is vibrating.

"Yeah," Ruben says, "just give her the cancer rap."

"Okay, okay," I say. "I don't want to get my face blown off. Try not to get yours blown off either."

"Hey, man, we won't," Angel says, dangling the toothpick from his mouth. He winks at me again, but to the side, so Ruben won't see it.

"Hey, believe me, Angel, I won't miss *you* if you're gone," I say.

"Sure you will, baby," he says, but Ruben's already got him by the sleeve, pushing him into the living room with warnings to leave me alone.

Even though we're all friends, basically both Ruben and I agree that Angel's a necessary creep. He's loyal as glue, and we've all lived on the same block our whole lives. The way Ruben tells it, Angel gives us a sense of history about ourselves.

"How come you're wearing colors?" I ask, watching them zip up their black and green Dragon jackets. That's the gang they belong to this year. Last year, they were Lords. The year before that, they were Rangers. Every time there's a turf war, the same little group of guys in the neighborhood switches

gangs to survive. They belong to whoever raises their
flag. In a year or two, we figure some new guys will
be dressing Freddy.

"Hey, baby, it's cold out there," Angel says, but
I'm not convinced. "Anyway, these are school colors.
Go team, go."

Not that he'd know anything about school. Angel
dropped out this past year, not so much because he
wanted to but because the school just wouldn't have
him anymore.

Now Ruben's fooling around with whatever's
under his shirt, shifting his pants, pulling on his belt.
"I thought you had homework," he says to me.

"I do."

"Well, get to it." He's a little cold; Ruben can do
that. He doesn't mean to be hurtful but it's the only
way he can manage sometimes. I shuffle back to the
dining room, which is really just an extension of the
kitchen, and I noisily open one of my books. I can
hear Angel rustling around the curtains.

"Fuck, man," he whispers loudly. "Goddam Lords
are out there. Look." Ruben turns the lights off and
steps to the window. I just sit, eyes locked on my
textbook, even in the dark. Freddy's in the back
bedroom, fast asleep.

"Well, okay, we'll wait," Ruben says. "I'm going
to call Tyrone. You stay down, all right?" He comes
around to the kitchen phone and dials, but he won't
look at me. "Hey Estela, why don't you sit on the
other side of the table, okay?" He wants me to move,
to not have my back to the front of the house. I just
do it, no argument. "Tyrone, man, what's going on?
We've got a mess of Lords sitting in front of my crib.
. . . Shit, yes . . . And my mom's gonna be home in
an hour."

"Motherfucker, motherfucker," mutters Angel from the living room. He's crouched next to the window, looking out through the parted curtains. "Somebody, man, somebody told."

"Told what, Angel?" I ask. Ruben's on hold.

"Told on us, squealed, that's what."

"Papo Velasquez's out of jail, convinced the D's put him in." Ruben holds the phone away.

"They did, so what's new?"

"Well, I don't know that. And even if we did, you don't go spill it all to the Lords. I mean, we're all Papo's got anyway."

I just shake my head. Papo's a thug; when he went up a few months ago, I was glad. The whole thing happened by accident anyway; nobody realized they were being set up when they asked Papo to represent the Dragons at a community meeting. The neighborhood association had promised immunity to gang members; instead, it tipped the cops and had everybody arrested. There's been nothing but war since then, with plenty of blame going around.

In the meantime, the young lawyer who headed the neighborhood group caught a bullet while hoeing his garden one Sunday afternoon. No one's been arrested for that, but the whole neighborhood knows it was a Lord. That's why Papo went with them. He's just mad, mad at the whole world, including the Dragons. And the only ones who are as angry and as crazy as he is—the only ones who are likely to seek revenge for its own sake—are the Lords.

"Man, they're just gonna sit there all night," Angel says.

"Look, Tyrone, I don't want those guys out there when my mother gets home, man," Ruben says into the phone. "It'll scare the fuck out of her. Just move 'em, you know, make a little noise on your end of the block." He pauses, feels the bulge under his shirt. "We'll get out of here, we'll meet you in the park, okay? We'll just go out my mom's bedroom window."

I'm thinking Freddy's in there, his breathing innocent and pure. Ruben hangs up, then walks slowly into the living room, his back to the wall.

"I wanna turn the TV on," Angel says, pointing to the huge Zenith cabinet opposite him. "It's dark enough they'll see the tube, you know, and think we're just going to relax and hang out for the night."

"Good idea," says Ruben, and he gets down on all fours and crawls to the set. He switches it on, but turns the volume off.

"How about some comedy, huh?" He flips the channels, settling on a "M*A*S*H" rerun.

I turn the pages of my book. It's the only sound we hear as we sit together, waiting for the Lords, or for Tyrone down the block to make a move.

"Somebody had to tell, Ruben," Angel whispers. His voice is awfully small now.

"I know."

"Tell what?" I ask.

Ruben looks up at me, his eyelashes fluttering. He's got a little fuzz on his lip and a stubble on his chin but right now he looks like baby Freddy's twin. He doesn't want to say anything, but since it's me who's asking, he'll tell all. "We was gonna go looking for Papo."

"What for?"

"Just to talk to him, you know."

I sigh. "He never was one for listening."

"Well, you know, I think he would have listened."

"Yeah?"

"Yeah, 'cause at one time, we were great friends. You know, since before the D's. And I think he just needed some reminding of that, 'cause nothing else matters."

"Except now, Ruben. I mean, he's got Lords all around the house," Angel says.

"Yeah," Ruben whispers, looking out through the curtains. "But I don't understand, man, I really don't. You don't double-cross the ones you love, the ones you need."

"Well, he thinks we double-crossed *him*," Angel says.

"But, see, that doesn't make sense." Ruben's face is screwed up in a frown. "Deep down, you know, he has to understand that we just didn't know."

"It's funny—it's not now—I mean, we asked Papo to go to that meeting for us 'cause we respected him so much," says Angel.

"And 'cause we knew him, and he knew us," Ruben adds.

Suddenly we all hear the noise at the same time, a kind of fumbling in the back of the house. I'm thinking of Freddy and I'm up, reckless about what can be seen or heard outside. But Angel, of all people, beats me to the back bedroom, patting down the bed for Freddy, then looking under it.

"Hey Freddy," Ruben says behind us. He's standing at the bathroom door, trying to stay loose, smiling.

Angel and I rush to him. Little Freddy's got a hand inside his pants, but the other is signaling for quiet with a gesture across his mouth. It's dark but his look is mischievous. Angel and I glance at each other, relieved. I can hear my heart beating right in my ears; Angel's chest is pumping.

"What's the matter, baby boy?" Ruben whispers, calmly squatting to meet him.

But Freddy dismisses him again, turning his attention instead to something under the clawfeet of our old bathtub. Ruben drops to his knees and crawls closer to Freddy; he's looking into the bleak corner when we hear a familiar squeal.

"More mice?" asks Angel, scowling.

I can't see a thing in the dark of the bathroom, with Freddy fascinated and Ruben on the floor. Everything is so cramped and shadowy. All I can think of is that I've never had to put a trap in the bathroom; I'll need to go to the store to buy more.

Then Angel reaches across my face to the light switch and turns it on. Freddy shrieks, scurrying into Ruben's arms. Angel's face turns a yellowish green. A small grey mouse is standing right under the tub, it's front legs waving in the air, while the remains of a second mouse lie next to him. Blood clings to his mouth and fur.

"That's disgusting," Angel says, taking the toothpick out of his mouth as he reaches over to turn the light off.

"Angel, don't be stupid," I say, pushing his arm away.

Ruben has Freddy off the floor instantly, then he steps up to the live mouse and stomps his foot in front of it, scaring it away.

"Whatcha doing, huh, Freddy?" he asks, but it's not a scolding. Ruben's being kind of sweet. "You just wanted to pee, I bet, is that it? Then these goddam mice got everywhere."

"That's so disgusting, man, so disgusting," Angel keeps saying.

As I go for my mouse gloves and something to clean up with, I notice Angel's holding his stomach. "Are you all right?"

"It makes me sick. Doesn't it make you sick?" His face is still turning colors.

I shrug. I mean, I'm kind of used to it. "Well, I've never cleaned up after a mouse that died without a trap," I say. I can hear Freddy peeing and Ruben taking him back to bed.

"It happens all the time," Angel says. "Mice go bananas and just eat each other alive."

I chuckle as I grab my gloves, a roll of paper towels and a bottle of Fantastik. "Since when are you such a mouse expert?"

"I tell you, Estela, I used to date this American girl and her little brother had mice, man. He was always crying 'cause the mice kept eating each other up."

Angel follows me to the bathroom again. I pick up the dead mouse and flip him into the toilet, then spray the floor and start wiping. Angel flushes the toilet. "I swear that's gotta be bad for the plumbing," he says.

"Angel, what do you expect me to do? If I put it in the garbage, it'll attract cockroaches for sure."

"Hey, hey," he says, his hands flashing surrender. "I don't have an answer, okay? I just think the whole thing stinks, all right?" He gets down on the floor, bunching up a handful of paper towels and finishing up the cleaning. "Let me do it, okay? You do it all the time."

Ruben leans in the bathroom door. "The Lords are gone," he announces. "I guess the TV trick worked."

Angel's skeptical. "Or maybe Tyrone did something. We've been kind of distracted, you know." He gets up slowly. "I'm still not going out the front door," he says, paper towels and Fantastik in his hands. "Not for weeks."

Ruben chuckles, following Angel to the kitchen. "So you're just going to stay here forever?"

They banter back and forth about leaving as I wash my hands in the bathroom. Frankly, I don't understand why they have to go now. They already know the score. The only thing happening on the streets is trouble.

"Why don't you just hang out?" I say to Ruben.

"I can't, I promised Tyrone."

Angel's upset. "Fuck, man."

"Look, we'll go out my mom's window; will that make you happy?"

"Yeah, ecstatic, man, delirious," Angel says. "And how do we know the Lords didn't hear all the commotion in the back of the house?"

Ruben sighs. "You want me to go first? Is that what you want? I'll do it. If they're back there, they'll get me first and then you can just sit back and watch "M*A*S*H" until the cops get here, okay?"

"I hope you've got a VCR and lots of "M*A*S*H" on tape, man, 'cause it'll be hours before the cops get here," Angel says. "Mickey Mouse and all his little rodent friends will be feasting on you."

"Angel, don't say that kind of shit," I say, slapping his shoulder. I try to not even think about what might happen, and my mom says it's bad luck to say things out loud. "Are you crazy?"

"Sure," he says, shaking his head, "I'm crazy—I'm the one."

"Let's go," Ruben says, grabbing his sleeve again.

"I'm coming, I'm coming."

I follow them both to the back bedroom where
Freddy's lying under the covers wide awake. "Where
you going, Ruben?" he asks as our older brother
steps up on the bed and undoes the lock on the
window.

"Out," Ruben says, winking at him.

"You've got a gun," Freddy says.

Ruben continues his fiddling with the window but
Angel gives me a surprised look. "Watcha talking
about, Freddy? You dreaming or something?" Ruben
asks, unsmiling. He's not making eye contact with
anyone now.

"You didn't know?" I ask Angel, and he steps
back, shaking his head. They've carried knives before
but not guns, and I admit, in my mind, I'd already
put the blame on Angel.

"It's a pistol," Freddy says, his face lit up even in
the dark.

I sit down next to him, pushing his little body
further under the covers. "Don't talk like that," I say.

"I saw it," he says. "It was in Ruben's room." He's
beaming with pride.

"I'm going out the front," Angel suddenly
declares.

"You'll be dead meat," Ruben says, reaching
across the bed and grabbing Angel's jacket. "Don't
do it." His tone is icy, an order. I stare at him in
disbelief and for the first time all day, Ruben's look is
a firm, sure gaze, but I don't like it. Freddy, who now
senses there's something wrong, huddles close to me.

"What's going on?" Angel asks. "Come on,
Ruben, tell me." I know it's going to be me who has
to ask.

"You go first," Ruben says, motioning Angel to
the window.

"Why don't you answer his question first, Ruben."

He's so tense. The gun is too big for him, poking out of his belt like a gigantic erection. "It's Papo's gun," he says.

"Papo's gun? I didn't even know he had a gun," Angel says.

"I didn't either, until he went up. He gave it to me for safekeeping, but then he decided we did him in. So now I've got this gun, man, and he knows I've got it, and he thinks we fucked him."

"Jesus, Ruben, don't tell me you were going to give him back his gun?" I ask, suddenly realizing why Ruben wanted to get to Papo so quickly.

He nods. "We were friends, you know; that's why he gave it to me. I figured, if I give it back to him, we're still friends. I mean, he'd have to know that." Ruben looks like he's going to cry.

Angel nods, but there's resignation all over him. He leans forward and pats Ruben's butt. "Okay," he says, shrugging. "Let's go."

Ruben nods too; in his case, it's an apology. Angel steps up on the bed and throws his leg over the window sill.

"Sayonara," he says. In a second, he disappears, landing with a soft crash on the cold ground outside. The curtain flutters and Freddy and I both shiver for the first time.

"Bye, Ruben," Freddy says. Ruben smiles in our direction, but doesn't look at us.

"Close the window, Estela," he whispers, and then he drops from sight.

I follow his directions, watching the two dark shapes disappear into the alley.

"When's Mami going to be home?" Freddy asks.

"I don't know; any minute." I'm debating whether to call her or not. I could save her a trip home.

"Hey, whatcha doing?" Freddy asks covering his eyes when I turn on the lamp on the night table.

"Checking for change," I tell him.

I open the drawer to where I always drop my extra coins and count out some quarters. I've got two or three dollars in my pocketbook. But I know it'll take about five for Mami, Freddy and me to survive a night waiting, hanging out in the hospital cafeteria.

A MOVEMENT OF THE PEOPLE

Mildred entered the El car with her head down and eyes averted. She scanned the aisles as though looking for an empty seat, but she was secretly canvassing the El car.

It was a game she played often. She memorized the faces, mannerisms and actions of people she encountered during the day. If anything ever happened, or if something "big" were to go down, she alone would be the one to call on. She would be able to vividly recall to the officers on the scene, ". . . He was wearing a plaid coat with a yellow, dirty handkerchief in his pocket on his right, no, left side. Officer, she was a gray-haired, stoop-shouldered woman with a topaz ring on her third finger. . . ."

She would be on Ted Koppel's "Nightline" explaining her method of total recall. Oprah Winfrey would invite her on her show and hug her saying, "Girlfriend, how do you do that?" She would smile enigmatically and shake her head. Then she would wink at Aunt Rose smiling proudly in the front row of the studio audience.

She slid into an empty seat while making a mental note of the snake charm on the neck of the man in front of her. She stared out of the El window and watched the platforms and people whiz by. The El slowed to a stop and she read, "Cathy sucks good dick!" She grinned and wished Aunt Rose was riding with her. She'd say, "Look at that, Aunt Rose," and watch her aunt's mouth drop open in shock. She loved to see her aunt's face when she was shocked about something. Still grinning to herself, Mildred was lost in thought.

"Hey sister, why are you sitting there smiling?" "Who are you thinking about or should I say *what* are you thinking about?" A tall, slender man with dreadlocks slid into the seat next to her. She could smell a faint trace of incense on him. Incense and maleness. A sweet, musky combination.

"When someone tries to bother you don't look at them," Aunt Rose advised. "If you on the bus or El, look out the window and shake your head a little, that'll let them know."

Mildred turned her head to the window with a slight shake.

"What's that shake mean? No, I'm not smiling about somebody or what?" he persisted.

As he slid closer, she could feel his warm breath in her ear. She stared at the platforms and people whizzing by.

"You got a name?" he asked.

Mildred continued to stare.

"Baby, am I so ugly that you can't even look at me?"

She turned slightly toward him to prove that he wasn't *that* ugly. And he wasn't. He had on one of those skull caps in red, black and green over his dreadlocks. His eyes were bright and laughing at her out of smooth, dark skin. His mustache and beard were sprinkled with gray and the V-neck of his multicolored dashiki revealed more sprinkling.

"My name is O'Kanta," he said smiling at her. "And yours?"

"Mildred," she whispered.

"Uh, Mildred, listen," O'Kanta slid his arm across the back of her seat and she could feel it tickling her neck. "Do you think me and you can get together sometime?"

She snapped her head back to the window.

"I told you."

The El slowed to a stop and O'Kanta looked out of the window.

"Oh shit, this is my stop! "Here," he jumped up and took a leaflet out of his pocket and dropped it on her lap. "You can reach me here . . . and keep smiling, OK?" He gave her a wicked grin and was gone.

"Don't touch it," Aunt Rose advised. "Leave it right there."

Mildred waited until he'd gotten off and the El sped away before she curled her fingers around the paper and slid it into her pocket.

She floated down the El steps at Central and bought a $2.50 bunch of carnations for Aunt Rose. She smiled at the toothless flower man and held her head high as she walked the two blocks home. When she came into sight of the brown two-flat, she reached into her pocket to feel if the paper was still there. It was.

She unlocked the four locks that Aunt Rose insisted would protect them from the scum of the streets.

"Millie?" "Is that you?"

"Yeah Aunt Rose, it's me."

Mildred walked into the front room and saw her aunt at her favorite post—sitting in front of the window watching the comings and goings of the neighborhood.

"Look what I bought you," she said as she handed the flowers to her aunt. Aunt Rose smiled as she took the carnations and stood up as Mildred bent down for their customary greeting.

"I fried some chicken and opened up a can of cream style corn. It's on the stove," Aunt Rose said.

"I don't like cream style corn." Mildred came out and went into the kitchen.

"Yes you do."

"No I don't. *You* like cream style corn. *I* like whole kernel corn." Mildred wondered how many times they would have this discussion.

"How anybody could like that dry whole kernel corn is beyond me," Aunt Rose admonished. "Cream style is better for you and that's a proven fact."

Mildred knew where her aunt got her facts. She made them up. She went into the pantry and got out a can of whole kernel corn.

Mildred turned to her. "Do you want me to make a salad to go with it?"

Aunt Rose nodded absently as she arranged the flowers. She sat them in the middle of the kitchen table and turned to watch Mildred accusingly as she opened the can of corn and poured it into a pot.

"I met a man today." Mildred said casually.

Aunt Rose's head turned excitedly toward Mildred. "Where? At the bank?"

"No. I told you that tellers can't talk to the customers."

"Well, you can talk to some when you're cashing their check, can't you?" Aunt Rose persisted. "You can give him change and smile, can't you?"

"Do you want to hear this or not?"

Aunt Rose propped her elbows on the table. "What's his name?" she said warily.

"Well, you don't have to sound so excited."
Mildred rinsed the vegetables in the sink and smiled.
"Where did you meet him?" Aunt Rose ventured.
"On the El."
"I told you not to talk to nobody on the El.
Nobody but a bunch of fools ride the El."
Mildred got two bowls out of the cabinet. "*I* ride
it."
"I'm talking about men, as you well know Miss
Fast." What's his name?"
"O'Kanta."
"What? O' What?"
"O'Kanta," Mildred said offhandedly as she
placed the two bowls of salad on the table and
turned the corn off.
"What kind of name is that?" Aunt Rose asked
suspiciously.
"What kind of salad dressing do you want?"
"What kind have I been using for 20 years?"
"I don't know, I didn't ask him." Mildred got out
French and Italian.
"What was he, drugged out or something?"
"What do you mean, drugged out?" Mildred
turned to face her aunt with her hands on her hips.
"Does he have to be drugged out to talk to me?"
"You know what I mean." Aunt Rose got up to fix
their plates.
"He asked me out," Mildred offered.
"Well, I hope you told him *no*." Aunt Rose sat
down heavily with the two plates.
The last evening rays of the sun filtered into the
Johnson kitchen and reflected on the two heads
bowed in prayer.
"Precious Lord, we thank you for the food we're
about to receive . . ."

Mildred quietly closed the door of her bedroom. She slowly walked over to the closet and pulled out her brown winter coat. Fumbling in both pockets, she found the wrinkled square of paper and smiled. Curling one foot under her, she unfolded the paper. . . .

"*Brothers and Sisters, Let Us Become United in Our Struggle Against Racism. Let Us Educate Ourselves Economically and Politically. Let Us Come Together as We Show Our Love and Concern for Each Other. The Center for Black Awareness Is Available as a Means Towards Achieving These Ideals. Classes Are Offered in Preparing for the GED, Counselors Are Available for Job Assistance, Voter Registration . . .*"

"Millie!" Mildred jumped up guiltily and ran into the front room. Aunt Rose sat in her chair in front of the television and pointed at the television.

"What is it!" Mildred asked.

"Ssh," Aunt Rose waved her hand impatiently and leaned forward.

"Sources in the black community are offering the name of Harold Washington as a possible candidate in the February mayoral primary. Washington, currently Congressman of the 22nd District, could not be reached for comment. Black voters state that if there is a high black voter turnout, Washington could indeed become a viable candidate in the primary. Here now with the weather . . ."

Aunt Rose relaxed and turned to Mildred.

"Did you hear that, Mildred Johnson?" she asked softly as she rocked back and forth in her chair. "Did you hear that, Baby?"

"Aunt Rose, what are you getting yourself so worked up about?" Mildred asked impatiently. She thought of O'Kanta waiting for her in her bedroom and wriggled her toes in anticipation.

"Turn the TV off, child, and sit down. We're gonna help get Harold Washington elected," she stated decisively.

"What? What do you mean we gonna get him elected? Do you know anything about him or are you just gonna vote for him because he's black?"

"Do you think I'm a complete fool?" Aunt Rose shouted. "Don't you think I know a charlatan if I saw one?" She paused and took a long breath. "Look, Baby, I know you think that I don't do too much of anything all day. You think all I do all day is sit in this chair looking out of that window and rock. Or maybe do word puzzles and watch game shows." She held her hand up to silence Mildred's protests. "And I do sometimes. But I just don't sit and watch kids playing, women switching and men cussing. I watch people and that's a big difference. I watch the looks on their faces when they think that nobody's looking. I watch the children's faces light up when their Mamma comes home from work. I watch they eyes get big when they hear the ice cream truck. Do you know that that's a completely *different* look? I see the beaten down look in a man's eyes when he comes home after looking for work all day." She closed her eyes and rocked. "I see plenty, Baby. I see the stuff that makes character. And I'm not crazy."

"And you see all that in Harold Washington's face? I'm not saying you're crazy, Aunt Rose," Mildred interrupted. "But can't we just vote for him? We can do our part by voting for him, can't we?"

"I just told you that I see something in his face, didn't I? We are not just going to vote for him, we're going to help him get *elected.*"

"What do you mean?" Mildred asked suspiciously. "I don't know anything about him. Unfortunately, I don't possess your powers of face reading. I'll have to read something about him before I cast my vote." Mildred stood up and started to go back to her room with O'Kanta.

"Well, while you're reading about him you're gonna be going around with me knocking on doors or whatever we have to do."

"And just what are we going to say when people answer the door?" Mildred turned around and looked at her aunt in amazement. "Are you going to tell them about the character lines on his face?"

"Well, since your behind is so smart, I guess we'll be telling them about whatever you find out."

"Aunt Rose, he didn't even say he was going to run. They just said that his supporters were offering his name for consideration. I mean, he's already a congressman, right? He'll probably just stay there."

"He's gonna run. He's from here and he knows that we need him. Trust me, he'll run," Aunt Rose said smugly.

Watching her rock and hum, Mildred was struck by how old her aunt suddenly seemed. Maybe some hot tea would calm her down. "You want me to make you some hot tea, Aunt Rose?" she suggested.

"Tea!" Aunt Rose's eyes flew open. "Baby, we gonna have something stronger than tea with all the celebratin' we gonna do tonight."

She grunted as she got up from her chair and walked over to the china cabinet that housed all of the Johnson family treasures and took out two heavily designed glass cups.

"What are we celebrating?" Mildred asked as she watched her aunt reach for the dusty bottle of Mogen David.

Aunt Rose turned to her niece. "Didn't you hear nothing I said? What are you doing just standing there? Get the record on!"

Mildred walked over to the ancient console and slid open the side door that held her and Aunt Rose's prized collection of blues records. She pulled out the favorite that serviced all of their wedding, funeral, party and gospel needs. Wiping the album gently, she remembered for the 99th time that it was time to get another copy. She wondered if O'Kanta liked the blues. Nothing else was played in the Johnson household. She placed the record reverently on the turntable.

"Here, Baby." Aunt Rose brought her a glass of Mogen David.

Mildred turned to her aunt and raised her cup. "Harold?" she questioned.

"Harold," her aunt answered.

They both stared solemnly at each other as they turned their cups up. Mildred walked over and started the record.

"*I Been to Spain and Tokyo, to Africa and O-h-i-o,*" B.B. King sang. "*I never once made the news, I'm just a man who plays the blues.*"

Mildred started out with her shuffle. Head bent and eyes closed, she folded her arms across her chest and slid across the floor, stopping only to slowly rock down to the floor.

*"I take my loving everywhere, I come back and
they still care. . . One love ahead, one love behind,
one in my arms and you know one on my mind . . .
but there's one thing people—I never make my move
too soon. . . . "*

Mildred turned to Aunt Rose who, never moving
from one spot, was doing her shimmy. Staring
straight ahead with her lips pursed together, she had
both hands on her hips, swaying from side to side. At
certain intervals in the music, she would slowly
shimmy down to the floor. Taking her left hand off
her hip, she touched the tip of her index finger to her
tongue and touched the floor whispering, "Caldonia,
why is your head so hard?"

Mildred slid over to her aunt and continued to
dance until the record went off. She opened her eyes.
"You want to hear it again?"

"No, Baby, we got planning to do." Aunt Rose,
sat down heavily in her chair and reached for her fan
from Wisdom Seat Baptist Church.

"If you get that wore out after one record maybe
you better leave the shimmy alone," Mildred teased.
"I could always teach you my dance," she offered.

"Don't worry none about my shimmy," Aunt Rose
snapped. "Any fool can shuffle across the floor." She
motioned for Mildred to sit down beside her chair.

Mildred walked over to her aunt. "Aunt Rose, you
know I can't talk to strangers," she whispered.
"Please don't ask me to."

"Baby, you don't have to. I'll do all the talking.
You just stand behind me with all the information,"
Aunt Rose said decisively.

"And where are we supposed to get this
information?"

Mildred looked at the red and yellow flashing neon sign that read *ay's Li ors*. "Do you think it's supposed to say Ray's Liquors?" she turned to her aunt, "or Jay's Liquors?"

"Who cares?" Aunt Rose looked disdainfully at the blinking lights. "Are you sure this is the right place, Baby?"

Mildred pulled her coat closer to her body and shivered. "No, I'm not sure," she snapped. "This is your thing, remember?"

She walked a few steps away from her aunt and pretended that she was all alone. She looked up at the building and at the people lounging outside watching her and Aunt Rose curiously. What should she do if she saw O'Kanta? Would he expect some kind of recognition from her? Would he even remember her? Maybe she could slip in sort of nonchalantly as if she'd been there before. She'd walk in and throw her coat on a hook and start stuffing envelopes or something. Her outfit was probably all wrong, though. Was her corduroy skirt and sweater too Establishment? Aunt Rose wouldn't hear of her wearing jeans this morning. What if she took her coat off and everyone laughed? O'Kanta would help her out of her coat and back away in horror. . . .

"Let's go into the store and ask them how to get to the center," Aunt Rose suggested.

"You want to get into the liquor store?" Mildred raised her eyebrows. She held out her hand to her aunt. "I guess we could always pick up some Mogen David," she teased.

Aunt Rose squeezed her hand. "I should say not. We've got more than enough at home."

Hand in hand, Mildred and Aunt Rose crossed the street and opened the door to ay's Li ors. Aunt Rose walked pass the lottery line and went up to the man behind the cash register.

"I think we should get in line," Mildred whispered.

"Why should we?" Aunt Rose's voice boomed out over the surrounding voices. "We don't want to buy anything!"

Mildred hurriedly stepped away.

"Excuse me, son," Aunt Rose put her hand on the arm of a customer waiting in line to pay for a bottle of Jack Daniels. "Would you mind if I asked this gentleman how to get to the Center for Black Awareness? My niece and I want to help get Harold Washington elected," she explained.

"Say!" A heavyset woman in the lottery line turned around. "Did he say he was going to run?"

"Yeah, baby," the man whom Aunt Rose butted flashed a toothless grin. "My man was on the news the other night and he said he was gonna run. That is one heavy brother," he nodded confidently.

"Ain't Washington a congressman?" The cashier stopped and leaned his elbow on the register.

"Yes, that's right," Aunt Rose broke in happily, "but he's going to leave that job and come here to be our mayor."

"Hold on and wait just one minute."

A man of about 60 waved his hand at Aunt Rose. Turning back to the cashier he mumbled, "454, a dollar straight and a dollar box."

He turned to Aunt Rose. "Let me tell you one thing," he said while stopping to tuck his shirt into his pants. "These white folks here ain't never gonna let a black man become no mayor."

"Now that's our problem," the heavyset woman in the lottery line broke in. "We can't wait for white folks to *let* us do nothing. If we want it, we gonna have to *take* it." She pointed to the man in front of her. "You are our biggest problem. Old-fashioned negroes like you who are scared to change."

"Well, I really don't think that age has anything to do with it," Aunt Rose said huffily. "*I* think . . ."

"Sho' you right," the old man broke in, addressing the heavyset woman. "I am your biggest problem." He turned and faced the line. "Everyone of you women out here screaming politics is going home to an empty bed. Frustrated—that's what you is. Trying to be the man, trying to lead."

He shook his head as he took his lottery tickets and turned to leave.

The woman laughed along with the cashier.

A young man sitting on a stool in the corner raised his hand as if asking for permission to speak.

"They gonna kill him," he stated. "And we gonna set this city on fire when they do. Aaron, you better get you some fire insurance," he said to the cashier as he looked around the store.

Mildred stood in front of the potato chip aisle wondering what she would do if O'Kanta walked up to her at that moment. She wondered if he was a vegetarian. She seemed to remember people with dreadlocks and dashikis being into health foods. She casually moved over to the display of nuts.

The cashier grinned and picked up the bottle of Jack Daniels. "I ain't worried 'bout nobody coming up in here. They gonna have to bring something to get something. You can get to the center through that back door over there." He indicated the direction with a tilt of his head.

Mildred and Aunt Rose slowly walked to the door.
They looked back questioningly.

"Go on. It's open," he hollered. "I know y'all ain't
scared, are you?"

Aunt Rose opened the door to a flight of stairs.
She began to walk down with a confident stride.

Mildred gripped the handrail and began to ease
down.

The basement was filled with crates of beer and
wine bottles. Boxes of potato chips and pretzels were
stacked up against one wall. Located on the adjacent
wall was a door posting the same leaflet that
O'Kanta had given Mildred. Aunt Rose studied the
leaflet. "Well, this is it." She turned to Mildred who,
poised for flight, was eyeing the staircase.

Aunt Rose took her niece's hand and knocked
smartly on the door.

The door opened.

O'Kanta looked over and smiled, "Welcome
sisters. We were just beginning. Please," he gestured,
"have a seat."

Mildred bravely glanced up and saw the bright
orange, reds and browns of O'Kanta's dashiki. His
dreadlocks were tied back with some sort of string.

Reggie Young

JUNGLE LOVE

He cried out in a whisper at some image, at some vision—he cried out twice, a cry that was no more than a breath—"The horror! The horror!"

—Joseph Conrad, Heart of Darkness

Everything we needed to fight the revolution, we learned from TV. Like how to sneak up to the cargo cars of trains at night without being spotted. It seemed like the white man was either so arrogant that he didn't think anyone else could master his ways, or he thought we were just too stupid.

We had taught ourselves how to crawl like worms between blades of grass and clumps of gravel. Being swift and of an upright people, we naturally could have darted up to the trains we stalked like gazelles—quick and soft—but the faint sounds of our streaking bodies might have been enough to attract attention. Besides, we discovered from watching Tarzan and Jungle Jim movies on "The Early Show" how a loud twig, lying anywhere, was always ready to scream under the most silent footstep. It would've been just our luck to have some old tobacco-chewing cracker watchman with wax in his ears accidentally look in our direction as he spit his juice into the wind. So we'd creep up to the cars on our stomachs.

Busting into railroad cars was a federal crime, but that didn't mean much to us. Gator, the strong man of our group, could pull the seals off of boxcars with

his bare hands. With him along, we didn't have to
carry tools. Me and Monkey Jr. were always on
watch. If anyone approached it was our duty to warn
the others and then take the intruder out of the
game. We had only been hitting the tracks for a
couple of weeks, usually after our People's Political
Orientation classes were over. A couple of officials
from the Party organized the classes to prepare us to
manage our own local Party chapter down the line.
During our meetings we'd sit around for two or three
hours listening to the cats from the Party explain the
ideas of Marx and Lenin, and discuss books by
Fanon, Mao and others. The stuff was always so
boring that we couldn't wait to get out of there. We
liked the idea of organizing one of the Party's free
breakfast programs in our 'hood, but we knew the
only way we'd ever come up with the funds we
needed was by hustling them up ourselves. We had
heard about some of the Party programs in Oakland
and other cities because a hippie-looking teacher at
school passed out copies of their paper in my
journalism class. I'd take and show them to the
fellows. Even before we started messing around with
the Party, everybody in the 'hood knew us as the
Black Avengers, so going around playing like we
were some kind of colored Robin Hoods didn't
surprise too many folks.

One night, the four of us went over to the
Sacramento viaduct and climbed up there. Gator said
we needed to change our routine, that it wasn't smart
for us to go up around Central Park every night as
we had been doing. When we got up there, I was
amazed to find that I couldn't see the end of the lines
of trailer cars even as far down as we were. It seemed
to me like they stretched out far beyond the

boundaries of our world, running for what seemed like forever into the darkness. I figured the front ends were parked somewhere beyond the warehouses on Western Ave., maybe as far as Damen, four El stations down from where we lived. But we couldn't start our raid until we got to a spot closer to home; that way, if we found something we could use, we wouldn't have as far to take it away. As we walked down the embankment, everybody laughed at me when I said the tracks were our equator. They thought it was funny when I tried to explain how they divided our reality because they separated us from South Lawndale, where only white people lived. They said I was taking that political mumbo-jumbo the Party cats were throwing at us too seriously. Nobody wanted to believe it was an idea I thought up on my own. But I knew that the tracks were a line of demarcation, like the ones the newspapers talked about in Viet Nam—they cut all of us native sons off from the civilized world.

Monkey Jr. hit me in the back and told me to wake up. He said be ready because Gator was about to open up some cars. A few minutes later, when Gator slid open the door of the second or third car he had broken into, Treetop's match revealed a stack of boxes with names on them such as Norelco, Sunbeam, G.E. and Singer. We checked out the stuff and then, with our faces lit up like Christmas, started celebrating—everybody, that is, except Gator. He was acting all business-like, so we told him to loosen up.

Monk and I were slapping fives and shaking hands every which way we could, but while we were playing around, something zipped past my ear and made a thud in the gravel down the way. Then something whizzed over Monk's head—it ricocheted off the broadside of the coal-yard building that sat next to the inclined stretch of tracks. We looked at one another. Neither one of us knew what had happened. My guts started jumping around my insides just like Big Momma's Jello.

"Be cool, fools, or go yo' butts home!"

It was Gator. He had a handful of rocks and had thrown a couple to catch our attention. He pointed to the door of another car. He said if something good was in one, something better might be in some of the others. He said the whole train might be loaded with decent cargo and he wasn't about to waste any time finding out if it was. He stepped up to the door and began blowing on his fingers like doing that made them stronger, then pulled on the seal until it popped. We slid the door open and Top put a match up to his already lit cigarette, making it flare. In the flash of light we saw piles of tires of various types and sizes. Top cried out, "Hot damn, I knows we can get rid of this shit nice and fast."

I said, "Yeah, we should be able to get a lot of eggs and cereal with this. . ." but Tree interrupted me.

He said, "Bugs, you talkin' some bullshit! Before I start feedin' anyone, I'm gettin' me a new tam and army jacket first, just like the ones them big time Party cats be wearin'."

Gator didn't let him get the words out of his mouth before he told him, "Forget that! You need some clothes, nigger, go get a job."

Top walked away saying, "Alright, big shot," but in a way that meant it wasn't all right.

Gator ordered me and Monk to start throwing the tires off of the embankment into the alley that ran parallel to the tracks while he and Top opened more cars. While we were hauling a load over to the alley, something flashed in my eyes from out of the darkness, making me go blind. I heard Monk holler, "Dive!" followed by the sound of his body crashing into the earth. There were other sounds of bodies scrambling but I couldn't see, so I couldn't move. The light held me frozen. Even after I closed them, my eyes kept burning like they were on fire. I couldn't get the light out no matter how hard I rubbed them. It was like somebody had taken my face and flung it into the sun. I dropped to my knees and bowed my head; then I heard a low, dry voice say, "Bang-bang. You're dead."

When my vision finally started to clear up, I saw what looked like a wild rhinoceros spring off his hind hoofs and charge into the air, but the light fell to the ground and I was once again blinded—this time, however, by the sudden darkness and only for a moment. I head the sound of flesh crashing into flesh and when my eyes cleared again, I saw Gator sprawled out on the ground holding Snake, the Party's Minister of Finance, in a vice-grip; a large lantern lay next to them. Then Shabaka, the Chairman of our local Party chapter, stepped from out of the shadow of the train.

"Ah, brother, brother man, peace. Peace brother. We just happened to be in the area and thought we'd check-in to see how you brothers are getting along."

The vice-grip around Snake's head tightened. Gator's jaws were blown up with air. He shouted out into the sky, "Fools done died for less!"

"Brother man, brother man, Minister Yao was only having a little fun with you. He was only trying to lighten up your spirits and cheer you up a bit. You brothers been working hard for the people and we just came by to lend a hand."

Treetop started spitting all over the place, the way he did when something made him mad. He started moving toward Shabaka, pointing his finger.

Monkey Jr. began rattling off at the mouth; he was signifying like crazy, but on nobody in particular.

"Mutherfussin' som'bitch mud'fuckers. You peebrainshitfacepusslippedskimpydickedassholedmaggotbreath sissies." Then he started casing them out with the dozens.

I looked around and tried to figure out what was going on, but I was lost. One moment, I thought, I was about to die, or at least get busted, but then I saw my partners attacking the leaders of our movement—two guys who just popped up on the scene out of the darkness. Shabaka explained how he had always planned to come around and lend us a hand, and since things in the streets were kind of slow that evening, he decided it was a good time to come and check us out.

Gator let Snake up and raised his fists in defense against any retaliation, but Snake didn't try anything. Instead, he walked over and extended an outstretched palm.

"For the people, brother."

Gator replied, "Yeah, bro," and walked away leaving the hand still stretched out in the air.

At that point, I noticed how really odd we were compared to the Party officials. We were high school kids, while those guys had long been out of school. They called themselves revolutionary warriors, enemies against U.S. fascism and conscientious objectors to the war. Shabaka had spent several years in college. Word on the street said that Snake had spent time in jail. They knew about stuff that we didn't even know existed, and complex angles to things that we looked upon as simple. We wore gym shoes, blue jeans, and T-shirts with our old fantasy identities scribbled on them—Gator was the Incredible Hulk, Treetop was Giant Man, Monkey Jr. was Quicksilver and I was the Ant Man. Our hair was cut short because our heads had to look the way our folks wanted them, while Shabaka and his Minister of Finance both wore black tams over their bulging naturals. They walked around in combat boots, black turtleneck sweaters under green army field jackets, and light colored Levis. We had visions of romance in our eyes. Theirs were as bloodshot as the moon hovering over the Bluesville sky. I figured Party business seldom let them rest and that was why they always wore dark glasses. I found myself wishing I could be like them. We had heard all of the rumors about the Party cats dealing, but I, for one, didn't believe them. Shabaka had warned us often enough about how counter-revolutionary forces were trying to discredit our movement and that one of their main weapons of sabotage was rumors.

Snake was puffing away on a cigarette as he addressed us: "You boys have any luck?"

He was tall and skinny. When he talked his head bobbed around on his neck in a circular motion, with his long pink tongue slithering in and out of his thick-lipped mouth. He was so black that he was almost as dark as the shadows he stood in. He had a sneaky-looking smile that revealed deep yellow teeth. He looked like an unlikely partner for the ivory-skinned Shabaka, who could have cut his hair, put on a suit and become a pimp, preacher or insurance salesman without much difficulty.

Gator ignored Snake and then looked at Shabaka. He nodded his head toward the first two cars we had opened and said, "Yo." Treetop, still pissed, mumbled, "Don't show them assholes a damn thing." Monkey Jr. agreed, saying, "Tell them pussies to go home and suck they momma's dicks." Slowly shaking his head from side to side in a manner which indicated he both understood and sympathized with the way we felt, Shabaka waved Snake over toward the cars Gator pointed out. Snake, while sticking his head into one of the opened cars, took a pull on his cigarette—the faint flare-up of light from the burning end revealed the cargo we had discovered. He pulled a pearl-handled lighter from out of his jacket pocket, lit it and said, "Aw shit!" Shabaka ran up to his side and then the two of them started slapping hands; one after the other they threw their tams up into the air as if they had just hit that night's number.

None of my buddies looked so excited.

To Shabaka and Snake, the real find was the stuff Gator showed them in the next car he opened. It contained shotguns, rifles, all kinds of ammo and other explosives. To me it wasn't such a big deal because I couldn't take any of it home. Besides, our real goal, I thought, was to come up with some merchandise we could turn into food. Treetop agreed; he asked if we were about to start feeding people bullets. Shabaka, with one hand held up to his mouth and the other one folded across his mid-section, his dark shades looking up toward the sky, rationalized that we, as vital members of the Party, were in need of some weapons ourselves. He said that we could also sell guns and ammo quicker than we could sell clock radios, mixers, and toasters, and make more money. To tell the truth, I thought that whoever was in the market for that kind of stuff were probably people that the Party wouldn't associate with. The Cobras and the K-Town Mau-Maus were the only ones I knew of who messed around with guns and they didn't use them for any revolutionary purposes—they used them on each other. If you dealt with one, you became an enemy of the other. I tried not to let the talk bother me, though, figuring Shabaka knew best and whatever he said was probably right.

We loaded Shabaka's Mustang full of weapons and they took off. He and Snake told us they were taking the cargo to another Party cat's apartment near Douglass Park—they said they'd be right back to take some of the tires and electric gadgets. We were all sweaty and thirsty and since there wasn't much else we could do but wait, Monk and I decided to go by the 24-hour liquor store on Cermak and Kedzie to get some pop. We ran over to the Spaulding Avenue viaduct and jumped off on the far side of the street and raced along from there. When we got there, Monk stopped me before I could go in and pointed across the street. Shabaka was on the pay phone next to the old closed-down gas station.

Monk asked, "Why'd they come this way when they were supposed to been goin' in the opposite direction?"

Snake was in the ride smoking on something so hard, it looked like he was sucking on a straw. Shabaka's hat covered the mouthpiece of the phone. They didn't notice us. Monk was bothered, but I told him Shabaka was probably checking with the Party cat to let him know they were bringing over our stuff, or informing some higher ranking Party officials about our successful raid. I told Monk that it was too dangerous for him to talk Party business on the phone without muffling his voice, reminding him that Shabaka always warned us about the many ears J. Edgar Hoover has turned in on our movement.

We got our pops and headed back to the viaduct from the opposite direction, but when we turned the corner at 21st and Spaulding we found police cars blocking the street. A couple of cops had Treetop in cuffs and were stuffing him into the back of one of their cars. Monk and I turned and started acting like we were about to walk away when we saw a black streak dart across the street and into the gangway between the two building on the other side. Monk said, "Damn, that's Gator." Just then, a couple of cops came up behind us and said, "Where the hell you assholes think you're going?" They asked if we had seen any suspicious looking men running from the viaduct and we told him, "No sir." They ordered us to get off the street or else they'd bust us for curfew. We took off running, hollering "Oink-oink, oink-oink," as we ran away.

Despite the cops, we hung around close by; we had to warn Shabaka and Snake to turn around in time so they wouldn't get spotted. But they never returned. We reckoned they saw the lights from the squad cars from a distance and figured things out on their own. After waiting for nearly two hours, Monk and I cut out.

Monk spent the night with me. The next morning after we got up and went outside, we heard Treetop was already back out on the street. We caught up

with him and Gator over in the park. When we saw
Top, we were surprised to see that he was still in one
piece—Monk and I had stayed up most of the night
talking about how bad the cops were going to bust
him up—but Top said, "Brutalizin' me was the last
thing they had on their minds. All they wanted was
information and that's exactly what I gave 'em."

He said, "All they caught me doing was pissin'.
That's cause when Gator told me it smelled like some
pigs were comin', I tried to scoot under the coal yard
fence like he did, but I was too big, so I took to the
alley. When I jumped down there it was already too
late. So right before I was about to be spotted, I
figured I might as well take me a leak. At least that
gave me something to lie about. When the pigs ran
up to grab me, I was still doin' it. They told me to
turn around with my hands up in the air, but when I
did they backed off 'cause I would've wound up
pissin' on 'em. When I finished, they asked me what
was I doin' in the alley—I told 'em, 'Goddam, what
it look like?' I said the only reason I was there was
'cause I couldn't hold it any more and I didn't want
to act like a cannibal or something and do it out in
the middle of the street. Them pigs ate that shit up,
too. Then they asked me if I had seen anybody
comin' down from off the tracks, so I told 'em what
they wanted to hear. I said, 'Yeah, some dudes just
ran by me like they had just stole something.' Since I
didn't know nuthin' else to tell them, I told 'em
whoever it was looked like they were in some kind of
gang, or something. That's why they took me
in—they wanted me to look at some pictures. And
guess what? The first faces I saw belonged to those

jive assholes: Shabaka and Snake. I would've fingered them suckers, too, if they didn't have our shit from last night."

Gator asked him, "Who did you finger?" He said he knew damn well that they wouldn't have let Treetop go without giving them something; especially since they had to know what was on the train.

"And you know damn well how nervous the man gets when he knows some niggers got some guns."

Tree shook his head and said, "Yeah, I know." What he told the cops was that the dudes he saw had on brown leather jackets and skull caps and that they jumped into a black car and drove away. Monk said, "Aw shit—you told 'em that the Cobras did it! That means they gonna be after us now!"

Gator didn't think so.

"Hell naw! The Cobras gonna believe the Party cats were the ones who fingered 'em to keep the heat off themselves. You know they think we ain't nuthin' but the Party Cat's flunkies, anyway. Besides, it ain't gonna take too long for them to find out we ain't holdin' none of the loot from last night." Gator stopped for a minute and started to smile, then he said, "You know, Shabaka and that boy of his are bad when they can sneak up on people in the dark. Now let's see how they act when the heat's comin' down on them."

We looked for Shabaka and Snake for days. None of us knew where they lived, except that they lived somewhere over on the South Side. Whenever we needed to get word to them, we'd leave a message with the Stamps sisters—before all of this happened, there were rumors going around saying they were giving it up to the Party cats in exchange for smoke and blow. Everyone knew they were getting something from somewhere because they were dealing to all of the kids at school, but I didn't think that meant they were getting it from our Party leaders. I figured somebody accused Shabaka and Snake of being their connect because they couldn't identify the sisters' real source. We went by there, but Brandy and Ruby May claimed they hadn't seen the Party cats recently and swore they knew nothing of their whereabouts. When time for our next couple of People's Political Orientation classes came around, they didn't show up and we didn't have any luck tracking them down in the streets. We didn't know what had happened to them and I, for one, thought it was our duty to find them and tell them what had gone down. Gator agreed with me, but only in principle. Otherwise, he said, he didn't give a shit about what might have happened to them. Treetop said he just didn't give a shit, not at all.

A few days later, the Cobras' black Impala started following us around every place we went. They had been picked up by the cops not long after Treetop got out, and when we saw them back on the streets I thought it might have meant that our Party chiefs had been picked up in their place. Gator said, "No way."

"Word would've been all over the 'vine if the cops had 'em. It would've been on WVON and in the *Defender*, too. Even the white press would've picked up on it. It's one thing for the man to bust some gangbangers, but when he busts some so-called bad-ass, black political muddafuccas, they always try to make it seem like they done busted Ho Chi Minh himself."

A junkie came up to us and asked about them, saying, "Ya'll boys must be lyin' low, waitin' for the heat to let up?" Gator, trying to play dumb, asked, "What heat?" He took his cigarette from his mouth, thumped the ashes with his index finger and looked at us like he knew we were trying to give him some jive. His yellow eyes got real big and his caked lips tightened as he replied, "The heat they gettin' from them guns they stole, nigger! Like you sissies don't know about that stash they traded to the Mau-Maus for all that reefer and blow."

I was confused. We were all confused. Our Party chiefs wouldn't have gone underground without contacting us unless something really deep had gone down. Their absence caused all kinds of new rumors to spread, even among junkies. Gator decided it was best not to discuss the Party in public until things cooled down. Treetop said it would be even smarter for us to not hang out together for awhile. We all agreed. We walked away from one another without saying another word.

I ran into Gator in the park later that week. We sat down under a tree and started looking at comic books, but neither of us did any serious reading. We both felt like zombies. All of the adventures we used to dream about having, all of the things we were going to do to improve our community, to improve our world, had turned sour in our stomach—like a stale funk that was making us sick and refused to away. Gator balled up my new copy of the *X-Men* and threw it against a tree. He said "The hell!" and asked me if I wanted to go by the Stamps sisters to cop something. He said we might as well—"Sure as hell can't make us feel any worse." Neither of us had seriously gotten high, but everybody else did, and, for some reason, we were the only ones walking around the 'hood feeling down. I told him, "Heck, why not," and we both got up to go.

When the four of us had gone by the Stamps sisters' crib the week before to see if they had seen Shabaka and Snake, they offered to sell us some Jamaican Red, some speedball, or anything else we wanted. Gator told them they were crazy, that that shit was death and we didn't mess with it, but now we were on our way back there hoping to get blowed. We had about three bucks between us and figured we could cop a couple of joints and a few red devils with that much money and then we'd go and catch up with Top and Monk.

When we got there no one answered the bell, but since the lock on the door was broken, we walked on in and up the stairs to their crib on the second floor. Gator was about to knock on the door but stopped his fist before it struck wood. He told me to listen up. I could hear Snake's voice through the door. He was singing, "OOO OOO OOOooooo, Baby, Baby," trying to sound like Smoky, but his hoarse falsetto was all messed up. We could smell reefer smoke through the door. Gator's eyes started flickering. He said, "Shit," and then kicked the door so hard that it flew open. We found ourselves looking at Snake's red bloated eyes. He had a needle in his hand that had a drop of blood dangling from its tip.

Snake got up and stumbled into the front room of the apartment. He walked like a child who was using his legs for the first time. He was modeling a brand new green walking suit along with a nice, thick gold chain around his neck. He was also wearing some high-top black suede platform shoes with red, black and green patches embroidered on the sides like miniature liberation flags. Gator took a long look at him and then started whipping his ass like he was Ali all over Floyd Patterson again, but Snake looked like he wasn't feeling any pain. I asked Gator, "What you doing; what you doing that for?" As far as I knew, Gator was getting back at Snake for the way he had spooked us on the tracks. Then Gator grabbed him by the neck and started asking him questions, but the words came out of his mouth so loud and fast that I could barely understand what he was saying. I wasn't sure Snake could, either. The next thing I knew, Ruby Mae walked into the room and started picking up pieces of partially smoked joints out of the ashtrays. Gator looked at her and said, "Is Shabaka back there, bitch?" She answered, "Hell no, sissy, and if you call me another 'bitch,' I'll take a razor to yo' stupid ass." Then she turned around and went back into the other room like there was nothing unusual going on in her crib.

Gator asked Snake about the cargo we ripped off on the tracks. Snake told him, "Be cool, brother—just be cool." But Gator yelled back, "You remember anything about a breakfast program, nigger? Do you remember the breakfast program, nigger? Nigger, do you remember?"

Snake started mumbling, "Ah, ah, you know, man. You know, man. Ah, ah . . ."

Gator told me to come on. Before we walked out, he yanked the shoes from off of Snake's feet, picked up a matching red, black and green leather jacket from off the chair where he had been sitting and snatched the gold chain from around his neck. Then Gator grabbed a black leather bag that he wouldn't have noticed if Snake hadn't told us not to mess with it. As we walked down the steps, he opened it up and pulled out a plastic bag full of foil wrapped packages. He opened one and it was full of white powder. When we reached the street, Gator lifted a manhole cover and dropped all of the stuff down to the rats.

Gator offered to bet me that Snake was going to call Shabaka to come help him.

"Not only is his dope gone, the sucker's clothes got blood on 'em and he ain't got no shoes—and you know damn well a nigger ain't goin' no where with his threads fucked up, especially when he ain't' wearin' nuthin' on his muddafuckin' feet." He told me to come on, so we could get ourselves ready to deal.

Before then, I wasn't sure I understood everything that had been going on with us and the Party cats, but as we walked down the street, I could no longer find comfort in being so naive. I liked Shabaka, even if nobody else did, and if I couldn't like Snake, I tried my best to respect him since he was Shabaka's right-hand man. To me, Shabaka was our Huey P. Newton, our Eldridge Cleaver, our H. Rap Brown and our Stokely Carmichael, all rolled into one. He was the baddest revolutionary around. I wanted him to make the outside world fear us; that way it would respect us. I saw him as the one person who could teach us about *black* love, and *black* honesty, and *black* pride. He was the only one we had—the only revolutionary who bothered doing any organizing in Bluesville, a place where no newspaper reporters or television cameras bothered coming, except for when we found new ways to kill one another. Shabaka preached power to the people and the people was me. I liked it. I robbed trains. For the people. I was going to feed the poor and educate them. The people. I was going to be in the vanguard of the people's revolution. But, at that moment, walking down the street with Gator, I felt like one of a flock of sheep, the people, who had all been screwed by our shepherds in the pasture. It was only then that I realized that I, too, just like Gator, wanted to get even. An idea hit me—I thought of how we could get back at them. If we were being watched by those who wanted to get at the Party cats, all we'd have to do is confront them, draw them out into the open, and then hold our ground. After that, whatever went down was their business. I told Gator about it and he liked it. He said it sounded like a plan to him. So we hurried off to get Monk and Top, figuring they'd want to be in on the action.

Shabaka pulled up in his car. When he got out we could see he was wearing new threads like the ones Snake had. His dark shades covered his eyes. If he saw the four of us sitting on a porch on the other side of the street, he didn't act like it. He pulled a garment bag out of the car. The street had gotten dark as dusk threw its shadow over the city. Shabaka's movements under the street lamp next to his car looked like those made by a person submerged in water. Treetop said, "This asshole must be as fucked up as ya'll said Snake was."

Top wanted to go run over there and get him right then, but Gator said, "Let's not act foolish—just go along with June Bug's plan. You know if we stay cool, we ain't gonna have to do a thing. Let's just wait!"

Me and Monk sneaked across the street and let the air out of Shabaka's tires after he went upstairs to the apartment. That way, we knew they wouldn't be taking off anytime soon. When the two of them walked out with their heads stuck down inside of their up-turned collars, we came down from our perches and walked toward the street. They reached the curb on their side of the street about the same time we reached ours. Treetop was spitting his head off. Monkey Jr. started signifying like crazy under his breath. Gator punched his right fist into his opened left palm. Shabaka noticed the deflated front tires and a big three dollar smile lit up his face. As he stood in front of his ride, a car with no lights turned the corner at the far end of the block and started creeping down the street in our direction. We kept our eyes focused on Shabaka, figuring he'd make his way to the rear of the car, but he didn't make a move to go in the trunk like we expected.

With all of us checking out Shabaka, nobody paid any attention to Snake, standing half-hidden on the other side of the car. But when I heard the sound of a zipper opening, I knew it was the garment bag, even though I couldn't see it. I had told myself I wasn't gonna be the one caught off guard this time. I yelled, "Down, ya'll!" as soon as I spotted the shortened barrel of the shotgun. By the time Snake raised it up to his eye, I was already in back of a car and everybody else was also taking cover.

Snake fired a shot. A windshield exploded and glass fragments started raining everywhere. I heard the sound of Shabaka's trunk opening; he was in the process of pulling out another weapon. On my fingertips and toes, I crawled to the end of the car, ready to make a dash to get away. I was afraid my big idea wasn't going to turn out as smart as I thought it was. Peeping around the car's fender, I could see that the two Party cats were ready to cross the street with their weapons pointed, but the car that had been approaching was now only a couple of car-lengths away. They started waving their arms, yelling for it to "Get the fuck out of the way!" They didn't pay much attention to the fact that the car, which was now coming to a halt, was black. All of a sudden, the car's high beams flashed on. Both of the Party cats covered their eyes.

All four doors of the car opened. Wiry figures popped out of each, wearing skull caps over processed heads. They wore no shirts under their open brown leather jackets. They were quick and graceful—almost silky smooth. All in one motion they aimed their handguns and started blowing holes in Shabaka's and Snake's heads like they were firing BBs into watermelons. After the two Party cats fell, the figures melted back into the car and the doors closed. As we gathered ourselves together along the curb, the windows opened and we saw all eight eyes staring dead at us from the dark interior of the car.

A voice said, "You ever fuck with us, you die too."

The car sped away. The two party cats were left sprawled out in the street—the blood oozing out of their bodies painted the concrete a filthy red. We walked away, not really surprised at the gun play, but shocked by the swiftness of the violence and the sudden silence which settled after the blasts of horrifying noise. We took a shortcut down the gangway between two houses. Gator had to stop and throw up, while Treetop kept saying over and over again, "Damn, I didn't know it was gonna be like that. Damn, I didn't know they was gonna do all that"—knowing the city would eventually arrive to inspect the mess. That night, they interviewed the Stamps sisters on the ten o'clock news.

Contributors' Notes

TONY ARDIZZONE was born and raised on Chicago's North Side and was graduated from the University of Illinois in 1971. He is the author of two novels, *In the Name of the Father* and *Heart of the Order*, as well as a collection of short stories, *The Evening News*, which received the 1985 Flannery O'Connor Award for Short Fiction. His work has also been awarded the Virginia Prize for Fiction, the Lawrence Foundation Award, and two fellowships from the National Endowment for the Arts. He has just completed work on *Larabi's Ox*, an interconnected book of stories set in Morocco. He lives in Bloomington, Indiana, where he teaches in the creative writing program at Indiana University.

GEORGE BAILEY, editor, was born in Madison County, Alabama, in 1946. He received his B.A. in Creative Writing from Columbia College and his M.A. in English from DePaul University. He teaches composition, literature, and public speaking in the English department at Columbia College. His short fiction and articles on a variety of topics have appeared in the *Chicago Sun-Times*, *Fra Noi*, and *Exchange* magazine. He is currently working on a novel and a collection of short stories. He lives in Oak Park with his wife Linda and their two sons.

MARK ALLEN BOONE is a native Chicagoan who grew up on Chicago's Near West Side. He graduated from the University of Illinois at Chicago in 1971 with a B.A. in sociology. He is assistant editorial director of adult education for Contemporary Books in Chicago. On weekends he edits fiction for *AIM Magazine*, a Chicago-based quarterly magazine that publishes fiction, poetry, and social commentary.

In addition to editing numerous books in the field of adult education, Mark has published short fiction as well as interviews and other nonfiction. His first novel, *Reunion: A Novel of the New South*, was published in 1989 by Holloway House Publishing Co. He is currently working on a second novel and a collection of short stories.

Mark is president and co-founder of the West Side Writers' Guild of Chicago and a member of the Society of Midland Authors. He lives in Oak Park with his wife Cynthia and their two children.

MAXINE CHERNOFF's latest book is a novel: *Plain Grief* (Summit). She is also the author of five books of poems and a collection of short stories: *Bop* (Vintage).

EILEEN CHERRY was born in Toledo, Ohio, and began writing at 14. Her poetry and fiction has appeared in *Black World*, *NOMMO: A Literary Legacy of Black Chicago*, *Spoon River Quarterly*, *Callaloo*, and *Open Places #41*. In 1987, she received an Illinois Arts Council Creative Artist Fellowship and the Gwendolyn Brooks Poet Laureate Award.

TONY DEL VALLE teaches fiction, literature, and composition at Columbia College, Chicago. He is a freelance journalist, an English/Spanish translator, and a broadcaster. He has been awarded a Leadership and Dedication Award by the Chicago Puerto Rican Congress and the ICEOP Award for academic achievement at the University of Illinois at Chicago, where he is completing a dissertation on literacy practices in Chicago Puerto Rican communities for a Ph.D. in Language, Literature, and Rhetoric. His work has appeared in Columbia College's award-winning anthology *Hair Trigger*. His first novel, *Voices*, is now being considered for publication.

ROCHELLE DISTELHEIM's fiction and poetry has appeared in *The North American Review*, *Other Voices*, *Confrontation*, *Mississippi Valley Review*, *The Fiddlehead*, *Descant*, *Sou'wester*, *Rhino*, *Oyez Review*, and *McCall's*. An essay, "Women as Artist as Writer," was included in *The Creative Process: Ten Years at Ragdale*. The Illinois Arts Council has awarded her a Literary Award in Fiction and three fellowships in fiction. She is presently completing a novel. She began life on Chicago's West Side and learned how to say "the Twenty-Fourth Ward" as soon as she could say anything. While she no longer lives there, the West Side has never stopped living with her.

AARON FREEMAN—producer/actor/writer—is host of the new public affairs program "Talking with Aaron Freeman" on WPWR-Channel 50, and the creator and star of the long-running musical comedy show "Aaron Freeman's Do The White Thing," which is now in its second hit year and playing at the acclaimed Steppenwolf North Theater in Chicago.

Aaron was the first African-American essayist of PBS's *MacNeil/Leher News Hour* and was among the essayists nominated for a 1987 Emmy Award. He also reported from Geneva, Switzerland, on the first, world-changing summit between Ronald Reagan and Mikhail Gorbachev for the Tribune Entertainment's WGN Radio. His work has also been covered by or quoted in and published in *Playboy*, *Newsweek*, *USA Today*, *The Philadelphia Inquirer*, *M Magazine*, *Chicago Magazine*, the Associated Press, and both *The Los Angeles Times* and *The New York Times*. He is the author of "Confessions of a Lottery Ball—The Inside Out World of Aaron Freeman" and a veteran of Chicago's legendary Second City.

J. CHIP HOWELL is primarily a science fiction writer. He is a graduate of Columbia College, Chicago, an English major with a secondary concentration in science. His work has appeared in *Nommo 2: Remembering Ourselves Whole* and *Chicago Arts and Communication*. He has worked on numerous nonfiction articles for the *Science, Technology, and Communication Newsletter* for Columbia College.

JAMES McMANUS's most recent books are *Girl with Electric Guitar* (short stories), *Great American* (poems), and *Ghost Waves* (a novel). Excerpts from his work have appeared in *The Atlantic Monthly*, *Best American Poetry 1991*, and *New American Writing*.

ACHY OBEJAS is a Chicago writer. Her work has appeared in *Abraxas*, *Beloit Poetry Journal*, *Revista Chicano-Riquena*, and many others. She is a 1986 recipient of an NEA grant in poetry. She is currently a part-time writing instructor at the School of the Art Institute of Chicago.

IRENE J. SMITH is a founding member and secretary of the West Side Writers' Guild, Inc. She received her B.A. from Roosevelt University and is a former editor for a local trade magazine. Irene is a native Chicagoan who grew up in the Garfield Park area and attended Providence St. Mel High School. "A Movement of the People" is an excerpt from her novel in progress. Irene currently resides in Oak Park.

DIANE WILLIAMS teaches adults who are returning to school at the Austin Career Education Center. Her prose and poetry have been published in magazines including the *Columbia Review*, *Chiron Review*, and *Common Lives*. Her first chapbook, *The Color of Enlightment*, is published by New Sins Press.

S.L. WISENBERG was born and raised in Houston, Texas, and came north in 1974 to study journalism at Northwestern University. She has an M.F.A. in English from the University of Iowa Writers' Workshop and has worked as a reporter for the *Miami Herald*. Her work has been published in *The New Yorker*, *Chicago Reader*, *Kenyon Review*, *Whole Earth Review*, *Tikkun*, *Naming the Daytime Moon: Stories and Poems by Chicago Women*, *Benchmark: Anthology of Contemporary Illinois Poetry*, and other newspapers, magazines, and anthologies. Wisenberg has won two Illinois Arts Council Literary Awards for stories in *Another Chicago Magazine* and *Other Voices* and was a 1990-91 writing Fellow at the Fine Arts Work Center in Provincetown, Massachusetts. She is a member of the Feminist Writers Guild and Network 44, a progressive organization in the 44th Ward on the North Side. She teaches at the School of the Art Institute of Chicago. She has work forthcoming in the *North American Review* and a poetry anthology, *What's a Nice Girl Like You Doing in a Relationship Like This?* (Crossing Press). This nonfiction piece was originally read on WBEZ-FM, Chicago's National Public Radio affiliate.

REGGIE YOUNG grew up in the North Lawndale community of Chicago's West Side where he attended Farragut High School. He later studied at the University of Illinois at Chicago, where he earned a B.A. in Black Studies and an M.A. and a Ph.D. in English with a specialization in creative writing. He is currently an assistant professor in the English Department at Villanova University, teaching African-American literature and creative writing courses. His story "Jungle Love" is an excerpt from his yet-to-be published dissertation, a novel set in North Lawndale during the 1960s, entitled *Crimes in Bluesville.*